"You'r

Hearing J[...]d if he would [...]ily's house, to [...] pressed his splayed hand against her, laughter in his eyes—and Kali knew he would dare anything.

"Jesse, no...."

"I just came in here to say good morning," he said innocently, "and Merry Christmas." He lowered his head to scatter kisses over her throat and shoulders.

Suddenly Kali couldn't let him go. She revelled in the textures of him...the velvet roughness of his tongue, the warm pressure of his bare chest. Their lips moved in teasing, tasting strokes.

"Merry Christmas, Jesse," she murmured breathlessly between kisses.

"It will be—" he grinned lecherously "—later, when we're alone to open our presents..."

For my husband, Bill,
whose love and encouragement
make all things possible

Message for Jesse

PATRICIA COUGHLIN

MILLS & BOON and the Rose Device are trademarks of the publisher. TEMPTATION is a trademark of Harlequin Enterprises Limited used under licence.

First published in Great Britain in 1994 by Mills & Boon Limited, Eton House, 18-24 Paradise Road, Richmond, Surrey TW9 1SR

© Patricia Coughlin 1992

*First published in Great Britain in 1994
by Mills & Boon Limited, Eton House, 18-24 Paradise Road,
Richmond, Surrey TW9 1SR*

© Patricia Madden Coughlin 1985

ISBN 0 263 78914 4

21 - 9410

*Printed in Great Britain by
BPC Paperbacks Ltd*

KALI SPENCER SLID closer to the edge of her seat as she watched Jesse McPherson, the Long Island Bandits' star center, glide across the ice, positioning himself between his swiftly approaching opponent and the net.

The front-row seat gave her a clear view of the action, and she stared, mesmerized by the cool determination in McPherson's stance as he lay in wait, the game's final anxiety-filled seconds ticking away. Then, in a lightning-fast move that epitomized the style his fans loved—rough and tumble—he shot forward, passing the puck to a fellow Bandit while grabbing the opposing player's jersey and riding him forward into the boards directly in front of her.

Along with everyone else in the Colosseum's cheering, sell-out crowd, Kali surged to her feet. But as most other eyes followed the progress of the puck, hers were riveted on the scuffle taking place just three feet away. It wasn't a violent skirmish by hockey standards. In fact, watching McPherson, dressed in black and white, deftly maneuvering his arms and his stick, Kali had the distinct impression he was toying with the other player. Given the short fuses of most hockey players, and both teams' propensity for all-out brawls, the incident might have turned into something much more colorful if the final horn hadn't sounded just then. It signaled the end of the action and the continuance of the Bandits' ten-game winning streak.

For a moment the two men before her carried on their rough jockeying against the boards. Then—very wisely, in Kali's opinion—the center from the visiting team backed off, skating to join his dejected teammates as they filed from the ice. McPherson stayed where he was, holding his stick aloft in acknowledgment of the lusty cheers and piercing whistles that echoed through the cavernous building.

Kali savored the opportunity to study, at close range, this man whose finesse on ice had awed her for the past two hours. The vital statistics provided by the team program hardly did him justice. He looked taller than six foot two and heavier than one hundred and ninety pounds, but Kali was certain that impression had more to do with the skates and pads he wore than any excess flesh. No doubt the agile control he'd displayed while passing and checking throughout the game was rooted in the whipcord strength of a perfectly conditioned athlete.

She watched in fascination as he removed his bulky gloves by clamping the fingertips of first one, then the other between strong white teeth and tugging. Immediately his long, impatient fingers reached up to discipline the thick, near-black hair that waved over his ears and fell across his forehead in a soft twist. The tousled hair softened only slightly the overall impact of a face that was lean, chiseled and uncompromisingly male. Just one brief look told Kali that Jesse McPherson's ruthless strategy on ice might very well extend to his life in general.

She smiled, watching him accept with equal aplomb the avalanche of back-slapping congratulations and the free advice offered by the fans seated around her. This section of seats was reserved for the holders of complimentary passes, mostly friends and relatives of the team. It was obvious McPherson was on friendly terms with many of them, returning their teasing gibes with a lazy smile that sent his dark mustache slanting and climbing, it seemed, all the way to his eyes. Listening unabashedly as he spoke to a man in one of the rows behind her, Kali wondered if his deep voice always held that faintly gritty, very seductive overtone, or if the effect was the result of all that shouting across the ice. Whatever, she liked the sound very much and was slightly irked when the tall, blond man at her side interrupted by tugging on the sleeve of her sweater.

"Kali, are you still with me? I feel as if I've been talking to a stone wall."

Kali flashed him contrite smile number two, certain Glen would interpret it correctly. In the five years since she'd lived in New York City, she and Glen Taylor had shared enough modeling assignments for him to learn every expression in her repertoire...and to become one of her closest friends. Their friendship was blessedly free of the rivalry often rampant among female models, and from the sexual tension that might have marred a less blatantly platonic relationship.

"I'm sorry, Glen, what were you saying?" She raised her shoulders in a sheepish shrug. "It's so noisy in here, I guess I didn't hear you."

"It's not that noisy," he chided, his classically handsome face arranged in a slight frown. "If I didn't know you were a grade-A hockey nut, I'd swear you were falling asleep on me."

"How could anyone fall asleep in a place this crowded—not to mention cold?" She quickly raised one hand to ward off the smart comeback Glen was never without. "That wasn't a complaint—I loved the game and I thank you for inviting me...even if you did get the tickets free."

"You ought to try adding never look a gift horse in the mouth to that list of down-home platitudes you're always spouting," suggested Glen, chuckling. Then, nodding at Jesse McPherson, who was edging his way toward the team exit, Glen added, "Actually that's the man you should be thanking."

"You mean he's the friend of a friend of a—"

"It's not all that complicated," he broke in. "McPherson lives in the same building as my buddy Joe. He has no family here in the city, so he sometimes offers Joe his free tickets. Tonight Joe was tied up with a business appointment, so he offered me the tickets...and I made the mistake of inviting you to tag along," Glen concluded, playfully tugging a lock of her shoulder-length, pale gold hair.

Kali grimaced. "And you say I have a tendency to ramble on." A deep, rumbled laugh drew her gaze back to McPherson. "Do you think maybe we should try to thank him for the tickets before we leave?"

"If I can catch his eye," Glen replied, pulling on his jacket.

"Will he recognize you?" For some reason the prospect of talking to Jesse McPherson was sending sparks of excitement streaking through her.

"I've met him a few times at Joe's place, and—" Glen broke off as McPherson turned, the move bringing all three face-to-face.

"Great game, Jesse." Glen whacked him on the shoulder as he passed. "And thanks for the tickets."

McPherson smiled and nodded. "Don't mention it—I'm glad Joe found someone who could use them."

As he lifted one foot over the low barrier separating the ice from the concrete walkway, his eyes slid to where Kali stood, angled slightly behind Glen's taller frame. That second when his silvery-green eyes locked with her clear blue ones probably would have seemed perfectly ordinary to any one of the nineteen thousand people streaming from the Colosseum, but to Kali the moment felt endless and electric and—judging from the look of purely masculine interest that flickered across his rough-hewn features—Jesse McPherson felt it, too.

The silent bond between them was abruptly broken when the last team stragglers barreled off the ice, propeling Jesse along with them to the locker room. Kali was still staring at his disappearing back when Glen pulled her into the aisle to join the crowd slowly making its way to the exit.

"Are you working tomorrow?" he asked over the shouts and laughter that filled the lobby.

"No—I had the leotard shoot booked, but we finished it ahead of schedule this afternoon."

He took her arm lightly as they stepped outside. "Great, then we can check out the postgame party at Mulligan's across the street. Joe says it's always a blast."

Kali shivered, feeling the bite of the icy December wind right through her soft, black wool coat. "I don't know, Glen. I don't—"

"I know—you don't like parties," he finished for her with a disgusted sigh. "But this won't be one of *those* parties." The haughty, sophisticated pose he affected was so comical Kali had to chuckle. "See, you're laughing already, and you enjoyed the game, and I know you'll have fun at the party. All those rugged hockey players will probably remind you of your brothers back in Willow Creek."

"Williston," she corrected, knowing the blunder was teasingly intentional.

He shrugged. "Oh, well, I knew it was someplace rustic sounding. Come on, Kali. Do it for old times' sake—think of it as a chance to relive those golden days when you were a cheerleader for the Williston High School hockey team."

Kali connected with a light blow to his midsection, but inside she was wavering. Tonight's game had seemed like a longed-for touch of home, and Glen was probably right about the postgame party not being one of the superslick, trendy ones she took pains to avoid.

"One drink," cajoled Glen, reading her well.

"One drink," Kali agreed, deciding to surrender gracefully and letting him pull her across the street just as the light started blinking the Don't Walk signal.

She craned her neck as she walked, staring at the extravagant display of Christmas lights lining both sides of the street. From the enormous, painstakingly decorated firs to the leafless birch trees with their simple strings of tiny white lights, Kali loved it all. She'd never been one of those people who protested that the Christmas season started too soon or lasted too long. Although December 25 was still a few weeks away, it might have been the holiday spirit that had prompted her to accept Glen's invitation to party. She gazed around at the crowd streaming in the same direction they were; a lot of other people were feeling the holiday spirit, as well.

"Are you sure we'll even be able to get into this place?" she suddenly thought to ask Glen. "It might be a private party."

"Sweetheart," Glen drawled from one side of his mouth, "with a classy dame like you on my arm, I could walk in anywhere."

"Well, at least now I know why you invited me to tag along," she grumbled playfully as, true to Glen's claim, they strolled into Mulligan's without a hitch.

Inside, the lights were dim, and a heady undercurrent of anticipation rippled through the wall-to-wall crowd awaiting the arrival of the Bandits. In the far corner of the main room a rock group played, the energetic beat barely audible above the shouts and laughter of a mob bent on partying. Searching for a table, Kali quickly decided, would be an exercise in futility, so she settled for staking out some relatively clear standing room while Glen went to the bar for drinks.

When he returned with the club soda she'd requested, Kali thanked him and took a long sip. "Between all the cheering I did at the game and the smoke in this place, I think I could drink a dozen of these."

"Well, it's your turn to fetch the next round, and I think when you check out the line at the bar, you'll decide you're not all that thirsty after all."

Kali peered around him to where people now stood six deep waiting for drinks. "You're right—I think I'll just sip this one very slowly."

Glen gook a gulp of his own drink. "So what do you think of the party?"

"I'm not sure—it's so loud in here I can't hear myself think."

"That's probably for the best," he returned with a wry smile. "Your problem is that—"

Kali was spared Glen's latest analysis of what she knew he considered her boring life-style. A very attractive red-head a bit taller than Kali's five foot nine arrived at that moment.

"Glen, honey," the woman purred, stretching to link both long arms around his neck. "I'm so happy to see a familiar face in this mob."

One look at Glen's expression told Kali he shared the sentiment completely.

"Hello, Jenny," he replied with a smile from ear to ear. "I didn't know you were a hockey fan."

"I'm not," came the giggling reply. "I'm a party fan."

Kali hid her smile behind the rim of her glass, but Glen must have caught her muffled snort, for he interrupted his enraptured staring long enough to introduce her to Jenny as "just a good friend." That detail neatly handled, the two of them embarked on a line of chitchat even a child could decipher. In less than two minutes of listening, Kali deduced that Jenny was also a model, that she'd worked with Glen before and that her interest in him was strictly unprofessional.

"So do you feel like dancing?" Jenny asked him finally, slanting a hesitant glance at Kali as if testing the "just friends" theory.

Glen turned to her, as well, but before he had a chance to speak, Kali waved them off with a sweep of her arm. "Go ahead and dance. I spotted a couple of friends across the room—I'll just go on over and join them for a while."

Glen hesitated, obviously torn between duty and desire. "You're sure you don't mind?"

"Positive."

"Don't you dare take off without telling me," he ordered with the voice of experience.

"Yes, sir." Kali saluted. "And if I have to go to the ladies' room I'll be sure to leave a trail of breadcrumbs so you can find me."

Glen's response was cut short by Jenny's dragging him off in the direction of the postage-stamp dance floor. For a moment Kali stood alone, sipping her drink and debating whether to approach the two women across the room. To say they were friends had been stretching things a bit. True, they did work out of the same modeling agency, but aside from exchanging pleasantries when they passed one another coming or going, she'd never spoken to either one of them. It wasn't that she didn't like them, simply that the longer she modeled, the more Kali realized how little she had in common with other women who did the same.

At twenty-five, she had long ceased being dazzled by the posh parties and slavering male attention many of her colleagues seemed to thrive on. It worried her sometimes that by shunning most parties and dates, she might be overreacting, growing so cynical that she couldn't believe anyone could be interested in her for reasons deeper than a flawless complexion and a picture-perfect smile. But if there was a healthy social alternative, Kali hadn't come up with it yet.

A minute later, the question of whether to approach the other women or stick it out alone was taken out of her hands. A long, rousing cheer signaled the arrival of the evening's conquering heroes. With nearly everyone else in the place straining to get near them, it took every slick move Kali could manage to make her way, against the human tide, to the back of the club. For a while she did her best to take part in the celebration, dancing with a string of eager partners and joining in the impromptu cheers that made the floor vibrate beneath her, but as the number of empty beer pitchers grew steadily, she found herself spending more and more time fending off unwanted attention, until she finally decided she should go home. Now all she had to do was find Glen.

Kali's height usually gave her a slight advantage in scanning a crowd, but this was no ordinary crowd, and she soon tired of wandering in circles without so much as a glimpse of Glen or Jenny. Determined to add some method to her mad search, she headed for the farthest corner of Mulligan's, planning to work her way forward inch by inch. Off to the side of the dance floor was a staircase with a sign that read Game Room and a big red arrow pointing down. She decided that was as good a place to start as any.

The air seemed clearer in the game room, and the electronic tones of the video games strangely soothing compared to the din upstairs. Kali stood just inside the doorway, checking the room out group by group until her searching gaze was caught and held by the steely green eyes of the man sitting all alone at a table tucked into the far corner.

Jesse McPherson was watching her with eyes that held neither a smile nor an invitation. Yet the relative familiarity of him in this roomful of strangers brought a smile to Kali's lips, and she instinctively took a step in his direction. Thoughts flickered through her mind as she made her way across the room. There was no denying that the polite thing to do was to go over to thank him for the tickets, and the compassionate thing to do was to speak to anyone sitting all by himself at a party. Yet undercutting Kali's noble attempts to rationalize her actions was an unsettling, elemental impulse that had nothing to do with good manners.

Smiling, she pulled the chair opposite him away from the table. "Do you mind if I join you for a minute?"

The question was purely rhetorical. She didn't notice the sharp narrowing of his eyes, which suggested he might mind very much indeed. She was already sitting when he invited dryly, "By all means, pull up a chair."

"Thanks. As a matter of fact," she added, sliding the chair around closer to his, catching the light scent of a cologne more subtle than she would have expected from a man who struck her as a maverick...on the ice and off, "I think I'll move over here a bit so I can keep an eye on the door. I'm looking for someone."

"I'm sure you are." The glance he flicked over her before returning his attention to his beer seemed to Kali insolently unhurried, vaguely speculative and thoroughly masculine.

Confident that her hair, cut so that it fell in a silky line to her shoulders, was virtually muss proof, and that the rose cashmere sweater she was wearing flattered her, she still couldn't shake the uncomfortable feeling that she'd just been judged by some unknown standard and found sorely lacking. Either that, she decided, or else Jesse McPherson was so painfully shy in a social situation that he couldn't manage even the most basic small talk. Having battled her own shyness over the past five years, Kali had only sympathy for anyone suffering that plight.

Extending her hand to him with a smile meant to be warm and reassuring, she said brightly, "I suppose it would help if I introduce myself—I'm—"

"I know who you are, princess."

Kali didn't have to think twice to guess where the nickname, drawled in a strangely mocking tone, came from. The posters, featuring her looking ethereally pale in a full-length white mink, were all over the city.

She dropped her hand with a slightly self-conscious grin. "I guess that ad really caught your eye."

The responding twist of his lips was more sardonic than admiring. "Mine and that of every other man who rides the subway or reads a magazine."

Kali found herself twisting her hair around one finger, a nervous habit she thought she'd outgrown. Jesse McPherson looked even more appealing clad in a dark, open-necked shirt and black denims, but a whole lot less friendly. Her smile suddenly felt a trifle strained.

"Well...I guess it ought to sell a lot of mints, then."

"Oh?" His dark brows lifted a scant centimeter. It was more than enough. "Is that what you were selling?"

Kali met his gaze head-on, beginning to think shyness was not Jesse McPherson's biggest problem, after all. "That's what the ad says—Bently's Mints will make you feel as cool as an Ice Princess."

"I guess I wasn't concentrating on the words."

If the remark had come from someone else, Kali might have taken it as a compliment, but the steady, disconcerting look McPherson was giving her precluded any such misinterpretation. She began to wish she'd never moved toward his table. Remembering her manners with great effort, she bit back a scathing retort. "Actually, I didn't come over here to talk about me. I came to thank you for the tickets to tonight's game."

"Your boyfriend already did that," he pointed out, quite rudely, Kali thought.

"Glen isn't my boyfriend," she replied automatically. Something—the taunting trace of amusement that filtered into his eyes; the hard, unyielding line of his posture—made her rattle on with an explanation he hardly deserved. "Glen and I are old friends. He was the first male model I worked with when I came to New York five years ago, and he sort of took me under his wing. He knows I come from a family of die-hard hockey fans, so he asked me to come along to tonight's game. It wasn't really a date."

He took a long, slow sip of his beer. "It wouldn't matter to me if it was."

Kali straightened in the seat, eyes flashing like dark sapphires, her chin coming up instinctively. "I wasn't suggesting that it would. I was simply trying to point out to you that you shouldn't have jumped to conclusions about my relationship with Glen."

"Fine," he responded, his tone reminding Kali of the cool control he exhibited on ice. "Now let me point out something to you—you're wasting your time, princess."

Kali hesitated. "I don't know what you mean." Then the first humiliating thoughts of what he might mean took shape, turning her cheeks the same rose shade as her sweater.

He leaned back in his chair with a casual nonchalance that didn't quite disguise the latent power she'd seen so splendidly unleashed just a short while ago. "Then let me spell it out for you. I don't date models."

"Or lepers?" she found the composure to add mockingly.

"Given a choice, I think I'd pick a leper. At least then I wouldn't have to spend the whole night discussing diets and watching her recheck her make-up."

"Tell me," Kali countered, resting her gently rounded chin on her palm, "do you stereotype people of all occupations, or are models singled out for that honor?"

"In my experience models are in a class by themselves." His cool tone left little doubt as to where that class ranked in his estimation.

"Sounds as if you've had some rough experiences with a lady who just *happened* to be a model."

He ignored her emphasis. "Let's just say I've witnessed them...and the model in question was no lady. She attached herself like a leech to my best friend—a guy I went to college and was drafted to the pros with—and bled him dry...then dropped him for bigger game."

"I'm sorry," she told him sincerely. "That was a sleazy thing to do, but models don't have a corner on the sleaze market. She could just as easily have been a secretary or a bank teller."

"I doubt it. Secretaries and bank tellers don't seem to have the passion for good times and fancy presents."

It was Kali's turn to arch her brows mockingly. "Ah, I see you do typecast other occupations, as well. I suppose, then, that you're too much of a bigot to listen when I tell you that most of the models I know—me included—don't need to attach themselves to men to get what they want. We can afford to pay our own way."

"Don't bet on it. Some habits get mighty expensive to afford—even on an Ice Princess's salary."

The thinly veiled allusion to drugs didn't shock Kali; it just annoyed her. Maybe she wasn't close enough to the social side of the industry to know if the widely reported use of cocaine was true, but she resented having the effect of the rumors and gossip wash off on her.

"You know, maybe you do have good reasons for your resentment of models in general, but you're dead wrong— not to mention flattering yourself grossly—if you think I came over here for any reason other than to express my appreciation for those tickets. I come from a small town, and back there we're taught to be polite...even if we're not interested."

"I come from a small town, too. And back there we're taught that at a party a lady sticks with the guy who brought her...even if he is just a good friend."

Kali didn't like the way he drawled the words "good friend" any more than she liked his smug, amused expression. Fighting the urge to imprint her outraged reaction on the side of his face, she conjured up a smile as sweet as her eyes were frosty.

"I'm beginning to think maybe I shouldn't have bothered thanking you for those tickets. The truth is, Glen and I probably did you a favor by taking them off your hands.

After all, with your charming personality, it's a sure bet you don't have any friends to give them to."

His lopsided grin came out of nowhere, reminding Kali of the easy way he'd bantered with the fans. No doubt the man could be devastatingly charming when he chose to be.

"Maybe you did me a favor at that," he admitted, running a scorching gaze slowly over the half of her that was visible above the table. "It's not every game I have my own special princess watching every move I make. I can't deny that you're beautiful...or that I found all that undivided attention very inspiring."

Kali flushed. Unable to deny the fact that she'd spent the better part of the game marveling at his fluid grace, she settled for a tart "Don't call me princess."

"I'll do much better than that," promised Jesse McPherson, his lean frame drawing her unwilling attention as he stood and pushed his chair neatly back to the table. "I won't call you at all."

2

KALI'S TEMPER had cooled only slightly by the time she located Glen standing alone at the bar a few minutes later.

"Where's your friend Jenny?" she asked.

Glen shook his head with a woebegone expression. "It seems she encountered another familiar face in the crowd—some lawyer—and forgot my name so fast it made my head spin. Models sure can be—"

"Don't say it," ordered Kali fiercely. "I've been the victim of one character assassination already tonight. I still can't believe the nerve of that man."

He glanced around as if he was missing something. "What man?"

"Jesse McPherson, that's what man. That oh-so-generous friend of your friend." Kali launched into a rundown of their stormy meeting, complete with colorful asides and much elaboration on her opinion of McPherson's intelligence quotient.

When she finished Glen reacted with a long, low whistle. "I'd say that man's been burned bad by a model."

"I just told you he said it happened to his best friend—not him."

"People always say that. It makes the telling less painful."

"Well, it didn't make it any less painful for me," she snapped, feeling the tide of her ire rising all over again. "He did everything but come right out and say I was shallow

and self-centered. Then that remark about not calling—
as if I was masochist enough to want him to, for Pete's
sake." Crossing her arms in front of her, she glared at Glen
without seeing him. "Oh, I'd like to make him eat those
words."

"Then do it."

Now she did focus on Glen, with a look that ques-
tioned his sanity. "In case you hadn't noticed, the man
happens to be a lot bigger and stronger than I am. And I
wouldn't wager two cents on him being gentleman enough
not to take full advantage of it."

"Take it from a man," Glen confided dryly, "you've got
weapons at your disposal much more lethal than physical
blows."

It took a second for his meaning to sink in. When it did
Kali's eyes opened wide. "Are you suggesting I come on to
him? Do exactly what he accused me of doing?"

"Just to prove your point, of course," he assured her
hastily, but not without a trace of amusement.

"It sounds more like you want me to prove his point."

"Not at all. He said he'd never date a model—so you
change his mind by maneuvering him into going out with
you. That will also give you a chance to prove to him that
not all models are like the parasite who raked his *friend*
over the coals."

A smile tugged at her lips. "It would almost be worth
spending an evening with him if I thought I could get him
to admit he was wrong."

"That part will be a snap," Glen insisted, clearly getting caught up in the plan. "Invite him out to dinner and
then just be yourself. A few hours of such relentless
wholesomeness will have him eating his words along with
his dessert."

Kali shot him a disgusted look. "You make me sound like Pollyanna."

"You come close," he teased, then ran his eyes lightly down her fitted black slacks and suede boots and back up. "Not that you look the part, I assure you." He sipped his drink, giving her time to think over his suggestion. "So are you feeling up to teaching McPherson a lesson?"

"It's tempting," Kali admitted, then switched from smiling to sighing as the complexity of the challenge set in. "No. We'd better forget it. I wouldn't even know where to begin."

"Where do the guys who pursue you usually begin?" Glen asked meaningfully. Seeing Kali's interest perk up again, he continued. "You've certainly been on the receiving end of enough flowery compliments and grandstand plays. Why not put all that experience to good use?"

"I don't know..." Kali was vacillating visibly now, her blue eyes narrowed. "It might be fun...but chasing after a guy isn't really my style."

"Neither is shallow and self-centered," Glen pointed out, stoking the fires of her resentment. "Are you going to let him get away with saying that?"

Direct challenges always had a compelling effect on Kali. With her adrenaline pumping furiously, she forgot all the potential logistic problems—not to mention the possible humiliation factor—and visualized only the heavenly sight of Jesse McPherson eating crow.

Eyes sparking with excitement, she smiled a deliciously wicked smile. "No.... No, I'm not going to let him get away with it. Jesse McPherson doesn't know it, but he's about to have his consciousness raised considerably."

DEVISING A PLAN to reverse the time-honored tradition of male pursuit was one thing; actually putting it into practice, Kali quickly discovered, was much more nerve-wracking. The prospect of phoning Jesse to ask for a date filled her with anxiety...and an accompanying rush of sympathy for all the boys and men who'd ever called her for the same reason. Seizing any excuse to postpone the inevitable, she decided that calling him out of the blue would surely result in a curt refusal. Instead she would try a little "softening up" before making direct contact.

She tried explaining that strategy to Glen a few days later during a photo session for a series of health-spa advertisements.

"How do you go about softening up somebody like him?" he inquired dubiously.

"Off hand, I'd say with a sledgehammer." Kali was following the photographer's instructions to chat and "look carefree" as they pretended to be a health-conscious couple headed for the raquetball courts. "But seeing as I'm not willing to sacrifice twenty years to life just for that pleasure, I'm going to try something a little more subtle. You know, the old flowers and candy routine."

Glen shot her an incredulous glance as he feigned a few warm-up swings with his racquet. "You're going to send flowers to a hockey player?"

Max, the photographer, cleared his throat loudly. "I don't care if she sends him the whole damn flower shop—will you two stop looking like you're debating the world-hunger problem and start earning your outrageous salaries?"

"Sorry, Max," they murmured in unison.

"Are you going to send him flowers?" Glen persisted through the thousand-watt grin he was flashing.

"No—flowers have been overdone. I need something less conventional, something with a little more pizzaz."

"How about a bellygram?"

Kali considered that briefly, then shook her head.

"Stop shaking your head!" ordered Max frantically. "Will someone please fix her hair on the side there?"

Hair properly smooth once more, Kali gifted Max with a blinding smile and continued. "No. A bellygram is definitely out. He strikes me as the Neanderthal type—he'd probably wind up dating the belly dancer."

"I'm beginning to wish I was shooting the belly dancer," groaned Max. "Will you two try to think fun...games...relaxation?"

Kali rolled her eyes at Glen. "I haven't relaxed since I let you talk me into this harebrained scheme."

Glen shrugged. "Stress is good for you—it helps build character."

"Yeah, but what kind of character?" she grumbled, then devoted all her concentration to following Max's directions as he led them through poses in swimsuits and exercise togs, by the pool and on the indoor running track. When he finally gave the word that they were through for the day, her body was tired, but her mind still raced with half-formed ideas of how to meet the challenge ahead.

Later, sitting in the back seat of the taxi on the way home, she turned to Glen with a triumphant smile. "I've got it. Balloons."

Without lifting his head from its resting place on the back of the seat, or opening his eyes, he asked, "Should that make sense to me?"

"I'm going to send McPherson a balloon-o-gram—or whatever the heck you call it. It's the perfect approach...a touch of playfulness...beguiling without being overly seductive. I think I'll have it delivered to him in the locker room after tonight's game." She sat back with a satisfied air. "That ought to grab his attention."

"I have no doubt about that." Glen chuckled, watching her with interest now. "But you're supposed to be charming him into going out with you, not making him the team laughingstock."

"I will be charming him in a roundabout way, and maybe saving myself some aggravation in the process. I'm going to include a little note with the balloons... something sweet, but direct, like 'Won't you please change your mind about calling?' Along with my phone number, of course. Who could resist that?"

"Jesse McPherson," Glen said unhelpfully.

"Well, if by some chance he does, I've also got a back-up plan. I'll send him a message via a clown."

"That's charming?"

"It will be if the clown is me."

Glen looked aghast. "You're not going to appear in public in that—get-up with the pointed hat and red nose?"

"Why not? I appear in public in it whenever I help out with a benefit for the Special Olympics."

"That's different. You can be forgiven for acting like a fool if it's in the name of charity."

"This is charity." A smile teased her lips. "I'll be making the world a nicer place by converting a bigot."

Glen looked decidedly unconvinced. "I think you're going about this all wrong."

The taxi lurched to a stop in front of her apartment building on New York's Upper East Side. Kali quickly handed Glen her share of the fare and opened the door.

"Glen, I know this whole thing was sort of your idea in the first place, but I think it will require a woman's touch from here on. I'll keep you posted." Then, just before slamming the door shut, she added, "Trust me. I know what I'm doing."

FOUR NIGHTS LATER, staring at her reflection in the mirror of the ladies' room at the Colosseum, she asked incredulously, "What on earth am I doing?"

The balloon bouquet had been an unqualified failure. The night she had sent it she'd waited nervously for some response—if not a friendly phone call, at least a hostile, accusing one. Something. She considered the possibility that it hadn't been delivered, but a photo on the front page of the next morning's sports section, showing a sheepish Jesse receiving it as he left the building, put that theory to rest.

Reluctant to play her trump card so early in the game, she had tried her luck with a box of handmade chocolates in the shape of tiny hockey sticks—disproving the age-old maxim that the way to a man's heart is through his stomach. If obnoxiously cute gifts weren't going to do the truck, she decided, something a little less easily ignored was called for.

At first the manager of the Colosseum had been reluctant to sell space on the flashing screen above the scoreboard for a message of a personal nature, but when Kali had pleadingly explained that she and Jesse had had a lover's spat, he had relented. That night, when the Bandits played the Wildcats, the words "Jesse McPherson, won't you please call Kali Spencer?" flashed brilliantly at fifteen-minute intervals throughout the game.

The response to that neon plea had been resounding silence, and Kali had been forced to admit that the time had come to put in a personal appearance. Not that her own mother would recognize her in this get-up, she thought, fluffing the cotton-candy pink hair frizzing from beneath her high, pointed hat. The pompom that topped it off matched the purple stripe in the bulbous, satiny jumpsuit disguising her slender shape. Shiny patent leather shoes, a red ball of a nose and lots of pancake make-up completed the outfit she had donned in one of the cubicles here during the final moments of the hockey game.

She waited patiently for several moments after the final horn blared, giving the crowd time to thin out, then slowly made her way along a predetermined route to the home team's locker room. The stunned guard posted at the end of the corridor hesitated only a split second before waving her past with a hearty chuckle. She paused a moment outside the locker-room door, rehearsing her lines once more, then knocked loudly. The door swung open almost immediately, and a man wearing only black uniform pants did a quick double take at the sight of her.

Before Kali had a chance to speak he recovered. Breaking into a huge grin, he said, "Don't tell me—you've got a message for Jesse."

Oh, boy, do I, she thought, hoping for the umpteenth time that revenge would be sweet enough to compensate for all this trouble. She responded with only a sing-songy "Sure do."

"I see," the big man continued, stroking his chin thoughtfully. "Well, I don't know whether to invite you in or call Jesse out. Are you a she clown or a he clown?"

"I believe the word you're looking for," she informed him as haughtily as possible under the circumstances, "is clownette. And I'll just wait here for Mr. McPherson, thank you."

His taunting shout of "Hey, Jess, there's a clownette here to see you" brought what looked to Kali like the entire team crowding into the corridor.

Joking and chuckling, they parted to let Jesse through. He stood before Kali, moving his eyes slowly over every nervous inch of her while she helplessly did the same to him. Dressed in snug, faded jeans, his white cotton shirt hanging open, he looked even more appealing—and virile—than she'd remembered. Or maybe she had simply willed herself to forget his appeal. Or maybe, Kali thought with a disturbing stab of awareness, this unfamiliar, totally feminine response mushrooming inside her had more to do with the outrageous way she was pursuing him than she'd like to admit.

He had obviously just taken a shower. It had left his dark hair and mustache with a silky moist sheen. Even his chest, covered with a mat of black hair that narrowed as it neared his belt buckle, had a squeaky-clean dampness that Kali could almost feel. Taking a step closer, he stared directly into her eyes, and Kali had to remind herself that she was traveling incognito, that he had no reason to suspect she was anything other than a clownette hired to deliver a message.

She was standing close enough now to watch the tiny lines form at the sides of his eyes as he broke into a reluctant smile. Close enough to catch the faint scent of his cologne, and unless her imagination was working overtime, she could even feel the warmth of his breath when he spoke.

"You wanted to see me?" His softly drawled question was enveloped in the roar of his teammates.

Five years of experience as a volunteer clown for the Special Olympics Committee had prepared Kali for this moment. An equal number of years playing at being something she wasn't, in front of a camera, carried her through. With a jaunty pirouette and a comically exaggerated bow, she plunged into the song she'd prepared. To the melody of "Let Me Entertain You," she sang "Let me wine and dine you, let me make you smile." She had purposely kept this revised version much shorter than the tunes she usually rearranged to entertain children at benefit performances, and in a matter of minutes that felt like decades, she was down on one knee before him in a flourishing finale.

Springing to her feet amid thundering applause, she found Jesse McPherson shaking his head with what looked promisingly like an air of amused resignation. Pressing the advantage of having him cornered in a crowd, Kali strained to raise her husky voice to a squeak, and asked, "Would you care to send the lady a reply?"

The team, waiting with baited breath, didn't have to wait long.

"The lady," Jesse announced, barely managing to suppress an all-out grin, "already knows my answer."

He quickly shouldered his way back through the crowd, leaving Kali struggling to reclaim the presence of mind to clamp her jaw shut.

Not bothering to change into the street clothes in her tote bag, she pulled on her coat and headed for home. Settled in the comfort of her pale-hued apartment, she reran the whole scene in her mind, wondering what had gone wrong. She'd played her trump card magnificently, and only succeeded in moving him from irritated to amused, still a heck of a long way from interested and contrite.

It was, she realized ruefully, probably time to fold her hand and run, and yet after tonight she was more unwilling than ever to do that. There was something about Jesse that intrigued her, appealing to her on a level that transcended the tension of their first meeting and the ludicrousness of the game she'd been playing. Perhaps it was something as simple as the way he crooked his mouth into a smile of such devastating charm that it erased all the hardness and cynicism from his expression. Whatever the attraction, Kali found herself wishing they'd had a chance to get to know each other under different circumstances.

Well, she sighed, there was no turning back now. If she was going to crack his wall of resistance, she would have to do it fast, before she crossed that thin line between being amusing and being thoroughly obnoxious. Knowing she had maybe one shot left, she climbed into bed to sleep on the dilemma. It was there, encased in scented, daisy-patterned sheets, that the coup de grace came to her.

While ordering the balloons from Balloony-Tunes, Inc., she'd perused their menu of other services. Sandwiched between the singing telegrams and dancing bears was one that caught her fancy. It had struck her at the time as wonderfully romantic, and she liked it even better now because it was something she could do herself, a way to approach Jesse *sans* disguise. Of course, it was also a way to make more of a fool of herself than she already had. What did one do, she wondered sleepily, with imported champagne, fresh-baked croissants and strawberry jam if the recipient of the Breakfast in Bed wasn't in a receptive mood when you got there?

OR WORSE, KALI fretted belatedly as she stepped from the elevator in Jesse's apartment building at nine o'clock the following Saturday morning. What if he was busy entertaining another woman? Doubts and misgivings spun inside her head like a roulette wheel as she walked down the hall to apartment thirty-seven, an overflowing wicker basket in one hand and a dozen pink and white carnations in the other. She'd taken time over the past two days to see her series of overtures through her quarry's eyes, and she wasn't sure she liked the sight. Fueled by a burgeoning interest in Jesse as a man, her desire to be done with this crazy charade had grown to rival her desire for vindication. Now, standing on his doorstep, she concluded that the breakfast she'd painstakingly prepared was as much peace offering as ploy.

It seemed as if hours passed between the time she rang the bell and the time he appeared in battered jeans and an even more battered white sweatshirt with Cumberland High School emblazoned across the front. He didn't exactly look surprised to see her standing there...but he didn't look dismayed, either, and Kali took that as a promising sign.

"Good morning," she plunged in, her smile touched with eagerness. "I've come to the conclusion that you don't care for balloons or candy, so I wondered if breakfast in bed might be more your style?" At his raised eyebrows she added hastily, "I meant figuratively speaking, of course."

"Of course. It's a good thing, too, since I've been out of bed for hours." His mustache slanted upward in a way Kali found fascinating. "I would have stayed tucked in, though, if I'd known Little Red Riding Hood was going to show up at my door."

Laughing, she glanced down at the red parka she was wearing, then back at him. "It wasn't an intentional choice. Besides, you don't make a very convincing grandmother."

"You're right—in view of the way I've been acting, I'd probably make a much better wolf. I haven't been very gracious."

Kali had a hunch that was as close to apologizing as Jesse McPherson ever got, and she snatched up the olive branch. "No, you haven't, but I suppose my approach hasn't really given you call to be, either Shall we consider it a draw?"

Jesse smiled at her, an honest-to-goodness smile that Kali decided was well worth waiting for, and held out his hand. "I think I'd like that."

She lifted both full hands with a small shrug. "If you want to shake on it, you're going to have to invite me in so I can put these down."

"I'm sorry—please come in."

Kali stepped into an apartment that was clean but rumpled, the habitat of a man who liked doing almost anything better than picking up after himself. It reminded her of the place her two oldest brothers had shared when they were in college, and she had to fight the urge to dig in and start hanging up shirts and straightening magazine piles the instant she shed her jacket.

As if reading her thoughts, Jesse started moving around the living room, gathering debris. "I'm sorry the place is a little messy—I mean a lot messy, but I've been busy, running in and out."

"Don't apologize. I grew up in a house with three brothers. I'm used to the male approach to housekeeping."

"At least the kitchen is clean."

A desire to please infiltrated his tone, and Kali smiled as she followed him out there. The kitchen was clean, and big enough to hold a round table and four ladderback chairs. The stark white countertops and tile floor contrasted pleasingly with the deep blues and grays in the living room. Jesse hovered as she unpacked the basket, heralding each item with the enthusiasm of a kid on Christmas morning.

"I wasn't sure if you liked strawberry jam or apricot " she explained, pulling out a jar of each.

"I love both." Holding a third glass jar aloft, he eyed her quizzically.

"It's quiche," explained Kali, "or at least it will be when I'm through. The crust is in here somewhere. I counted on you having an oven, and a coffee pot. I also brought freshly ground Irish Mocha coffee." She lifted her head out of the calico-lined basket long enough to ask, "You are Irish, aren't you?"

"Just a quarter. The rest is pure Scottish." He laughed at her disappointed frown. "That's okay. Scottish Mocha coffee doesn't have the same ring to it."

"No," she agreed, setting the oven to preheat. "But I could have worn a kilt or something if I'd known."

"I like what you're wearing just fine."

The husky edge to his voice drew Kali's attention from the coffee she was measuring. She turned to find his eyes very green, caressing her with a look of blatant male approval.

With a self-conscious shrug, she swept a hand over the loose knit sweater and traditional-cut blue jeans she'd so carefully selected for the occasion. "Well, I got the impression you didn't care for glamorous blondes, so I figured you might like a frumpy blonde a little bit better."

The effect of his sudden smile was pure magic. "You'd have a hard time looking frumpy in sackcloth and ashes or even—" a glint of pure deviltry shone silver in his eyes "—a satin clown costume."

Kali jerked upright, sloshing the quiche mixture she was pouring over the high sides of the pie crust. "You knew."

"Of course I knew." He stepped in with a sponge to repair the damage.

"But how? The costume and make-up cover all of me. Even my friends don't recognize me in that get-up...and you'd only seen me once before."

"Once was enough," he explained softly. "All I needed to see were your eyes. If I'd never met you again after that time in Mulligan's, I think I'd still have dreamed of your eyes every night for the rest of my life."

Kali's throat turned desert dry as he moved closer, lifting his hands to rest them gently on her shoulders, imparting a warmth that radiated through her whole body.

"Do you have any idea how beautiful they are? Or how many different shades of blue sparkle in them when you laugh...or when you're angry?" He trailed the pad of his thumb along her jaw and sent lightning zigzagging all the way to her toes. "Or when you look all soft and approachable, as you do right now?"

Kali watched his lips form the words, saw them moving lower, and suddenly she remembered all he'd implied that first night. "I didn't come here for this."

"Shh." His fingers were tracing velvet circles on the sensitive skin at the sides of her neck. "If I thought you came for this I wouldn't have let you in."

Her eyes fluttered shut, and she felt first the sweet warmth of his breath, then the silky roughness of his mustache, and finally his lips. It was like her first kiss all over again, for never had Kali been kissed like this. It started with gossamer gentleness as his lips slid against hers, as lightly exploring as the rough fingertips climbing the back of her neck. Then the tip of his tongue crept out to tease her lips, tracing their curves and dips so that when she willingly parted them a moment later, they were already slick with the taste of him, and Kali yearned for more.

The kiss deepened naturally, blooming into an urgent, searching thing, an eager give and take of pleasure and demand, surrender and invitation at once. Jesse claimed the soft heat of her mouth with strokes that grew steadily hungrier, exploring each sweet nook and cranny, coaxing her to do the same. With her palms pressed flat against his chest, she yielded to temptation and let her tongue wander over the grainy surface of his.

The sheer sensuality of the moment stunned Kali. She felt surrounded by him...the taste and scent and feel of him, and her senses whirled out of control. She trembled against him, and felt a responding shudder pass through his strong body as his arms wrapped around her fully, pulling her close enough to be scorched by his heat. His breath, when he finally drew back to smile at her, was a ragged echo of her own.

Feeling a new degree of vulnerability under his measuring gaze, Kali smiled back a little self-consciously. "Do you think that oven is hot enough yet?"

As a neutralizing remark it was painfully obvious, and it made Jesse's eyes dance mischievously. "It sure feels hot enough, princess."

Although the words came gently, pouring over her like heavy cream, Kali stiffened at his use of that particular nickname. "I meant it when I told you not to call me that. I'm nothing like the woman in that ad."

Jesse touched the skin just inside the ribbed neck of her sweater, and his eyes darkened with wonder. "You're right—you don't feel at all like ice. You feel more like satin...hot satin...and unless you want bed without breakfast," he added, dropping his hands abruptly, "I think we ought to get cooking."

He watched, mesmerized, as the peach blush of her cheeks deepened noticeably.

"I think maybe you're right," she said, turning away. "After all, it's better to be safe than sorry."

Jesse broke into a slow smile as she went about the task of cooking his breakfast, her movements sure and efficient. Better to be safe than sorry? It was hardly the witty, self-possessed response he expected. But then, Kali Spencer hadn't been quite like he expected right from the start, and he had a hunch he was only seeing the tip of the paradox that lay beneath the beautiful surface. And she was beautiful...he hadn't lied when he said he'd been dreaming of her. Of course he hadn't exactly revealed to her how richly detailed those dreams had become, either.

Lord, if she really was the type who played it safe that would have sent her high-tailing it out of here faster than a five-alarm fire. And scaring her off, Jesse decided, watching her set the table with the black-and-rose patterned china she pulled from that bottomless basket of hers, was the very last thing he wanted to do. The amazing truth was that he liked the feel of having her here in his home...in his kitchen. Only one small detail marred his mood of utter contentment—the haunting sensation that he'd just made a downpayment on something he really couldn't afford.

3

CURRENTS OF SENSUAL awareness lingered long after the kiss ended, roiling just beneath their attempts at casual conversation. Kali was stunned. Nothing in her past, and certainly nothing in the blend of curiosity and antagonism she'd grown accustomed to feeling for Jesse, had prepared her for the depth of her physical response. She'd kissed her share of men in her twenty-five years—men who were more handsome, more charming and certainly smoother in their approach than Jesse McPherson—but none of them had ever brought about this stab of sweet desire.

Actually, Kali decided as her pulse slowed to normal, her response was much more than surprising...it was downright alarming, and her thoughts remained a curious blend of the dreamy and the wary as she finished preparing breakfast. That didn't prevent her from noticing that the episode apparently hadn't had the same quelling effect on Jesse's appetite as it had on hers.

Watching as he popped the last bit of quiche into his mouth with an expression of supreme enjoyment, she heaved her most philosophical sigh. "Well, there's another good theory shot to pieces."

He paused in the act of carefully wiping his mouth with the rose linen napkin she'd also provided to shoot her an inquisitive glance.

"You know," she elaborated, "the one about real men not eating quiche."

A slow smile creased Jesse's mouth, lifting the left side of his dark mustache in a manner that was extremely disarming. "Let me tell you from personal experience: real men who live alone are more than happy to eat anything that doesn't come from a can they have to open themselves."

"*Now* you tell me. If I'd known you were so undiscriminating, I'd just have brought along a few cans of any old thing. Next time—"

He shook his head, interrupting her in midsentence. "Next time, I'll cook breakfast for you. And you don't have to look so amazed—I can scramble a few eggs and burn some toast when the occasion calls for it."

Kali smiled stiffly at the prospect. "Maybe next time we could just settle for some Danishes and instant coffee."

Their laughter mingled, then faded as it occurred to both of them at once how very calmly and matter-of-factly they were sitting there discussing future breakfasts together. Feeling a tingle of anticipation, Kali sat watching him in tongue-tied silence. For a second she wished she had ESP and could know for sure if Jesse was once more seeing her in the other night's unfavorable light, but the expression in his eyes, which grew steadily darker and warmer, soon laid that fear to rest with a vengeance.

"As much as I appreciate all the effort you went to this morning," he said softly, "I think I'd find anything delicious if you were sitting across the table while I ate it. Which brings me to another little matter I'd like to clear up—the bit about my being undiscriminating. Where women are concerned I'm sometimes a little too discriminating...or maybe defensive would be a better word." He raised his hand, halting her automatic protest. "Like the

other night after the game. I wish I could chalk my rude-
ness up to the fact that the pressure of maintaining this
winning streak has the whole team a little on edge, but
that's no excuse. I was wrong."

"Another great theory bites the dust." Kali snapped her
fingers, hiding her surprise and pleasure by conjuring up
a rueful expression. "I could have sworn you were of the
'real men never say they're sorry' school of thought."

Jesse's chuckle was soft, pitched low, a masculine caress of a sound. "You're not paying attention, I didn't say
I was sorry...and I'm not about to." He reached across the
table and with one finger bridged the lips Kali had parted
to deliver a spirited soliloquy on his poor manners. "How
could I be sorry when my stubborn ignorance led to some
of the most inspired attentions I've ever been the recipient
of?"

"Don't you mean the victim of?" asked Kali, amazed
that she could string two words together when his thumb
was slowly brushing the hollow beneath her lower lip. A
thrill that was fresh and vital and totally out of proportion to the light gesture skittered through her. "Did my
overtures embarrass you terribly?"

"Hell, no. I'm the envy of the whole team. It didn't take
long after that message appeared above the scoreboard for
one of them to find out that Kali Spencer is none other
than the famous Ice Princess." His mouth twisted in an all-
out grin. "At that point, half of them suggested in very
graphic terms that I must be permanently out of my mind
not to take you up on your invitation to call. The other half
asked if, as long as I wasn't interested, I'd pass your number on to them."

"And how did you handle their requests?"

"Just forcefully enough that no man made the mistake
of asking twice. I may have been too stubborn to admit to

myself that I was interested…very interested, but I sure as hell didn't want anyone else staking a claim on you."

"You mean you really were interested?" Kali asked, smiling with excitement at the discovery that he hadn't been as immune to her as she'd thought. "Right from the start? From that very first night in Mulligan's?"

"Maybe not then," admitted Jesse. "Although I was plenty attracted to you…and as mad as hell at you and myself because I didn't want to be." Again, his smile came as slowly as the strong, tapered fingers that traced a delicate path along her chin and throat before falling away completely, leaving Kali sizzling and bereft all at once. "I've been trying to fight it, trying to convince myself that you're just like every other model I've ever met, but believe me, you haven't been making it easy. The moment those balloons arrived I began to suspect you had a real sense of humor and might not be quite the mindless, self-centered creature I had assumed."

Kali grimaced. "You sure could have fooled me."

"I guess I was just enjoying being pursued with such style." He lifted one shoulder in a sheepish shrug. "In fact, the only thing I am sorry about is that it's all going to end now that you've surrendered."

"Now that *I've* surrendered?" Astonishment raised her usually husky voice an octave.

"Sure. I mean it was obvious from the beginning that your scheme was to bring me to heel without making the first direct contact. I'd say that arriving on my doorstep with an offer of breakfast in bed definitely qualifies as contact of a direct nature." His smile and the lazy tone of his deep voice suggested he was teasing, but Kali didn't quite trust the heat in his silvery-green gaze; that suggested something else entirely. "The question is, now that you've surrendered and brought me to heel in one fell swoop, what are you going to do with me?"

Excellent question, Kali thought. And one she was going to have to answer for herself sometime very soon. At first, all she had wanted from the smug, derisive Jesse McPherson was a little soul-satisfying revenge. But her goal had changed somewhere along the way—sometime between the chocolate hockey sticks and this moment that shimmered with the brand-new sensation his fingers had stroked into the silky skin of her throat—the burning desire to see him eat crow had given way to a far more complicated one.

The Jesse McPherson who sat there watching her with an undisguised blend of longing and apprehension made it easy to forget how smug and derisive he could be, and Kali had a hunch that forgetting that would be a fatal mistake. Still, when he unleashed that boyish grin, she felt he was possibly the most desirable, thought-jumbling man she'd ever met. Which brought her right back to his original question: what in the world was she going to do with him?

For the time being, she elected to skirt the issue. Flashing him the regal look that had sold a million mints, she deftly snatched a dish towel from the counter beside her. "What am I going to do with you? Why, the dishes, of course. What else?"

With indulgent good humor, Jesse allowed himself to be steered off the highly charged path their conversation had taken. He caught in midair the dish towel she fired at him. Kali washed while he dried, hiding a smile at the discovery that he approached dishes with the same lick-and-a-promise technique as he did housework. The conversation moved easily from one topic to another as they worked their way through the cups and plates, coming around to their shared interest in hockey just as she submerged the empty pie plate in a cloud of lemon-scented suds.

"I suspect Williston High School was probably just as hockey oriented as Cumberland High was," Jesse remarked, resting one lean hip against the counter while she scoured at a bit of baked-on piecrust.

"Maybe more so. I remember my mother complaining that when she wasn't watching one of my brothers playing hockey, she was listen—" She broke off and swung her gaze from the sink to his sweatshirt, then higher to his expression of guileless curiosity. Tapping the words emblazoned on his shirt with one wet fingertip, she said, "I think it's pretty obvious where you went to high school, but how did you know I came from Williston?"

A dark red flush suffused his cheeks. That was absolutely the last reaction Kali had expected from this man, and it charmed her all the way to her core.

"I don't know." He shrugged. "I guess you must have mentioned it."

"Uh-uh. No way. Five years of listening to New Yorkers' comments about the quaintness of my hometown have taught me not to mention Williston unless asked directly."

"I'm not a New Yorker."

"You're also not getting off the hook that easily. How did you know where I come from?"

He smiled, sending his mustache slanting. "I guess it must have been my friend Joe who mentioned it."

"Joe? You mean Glen's friend Joe? The one who lives in this building?"

Jesse nodded and reached for the clean pie plate, which Kali, preoccupied with her thoughts, resubmerged out of his reach at the last second.

"Why would Joe tell you a thing like that?"

"We were just talking."

She started to hand him the pie plate once more, mulling that over, then abruptly lowered it just as his reaching fingers grazed the side. "Nice try, McPherson, but how would Joe know what hometown I come from? He doesn't even know me."

"Maybe Glen told him." At the sight of Kali's blatantly disbelieving expression, he let his hopeful words end on a heavy sigh. "Then again maybe Glen told him after I asked Joe to pump him for all he could find about you." He stared at her with an expression that was an uncomfortable mingling of sheepish concern and embarrassed guilt. "Well, I had to know if Glen really was just a *friend*, didn't I?"

Kali managed to look righteously indignant for a grand total of ten seconds before giving in to appreciative laughter bubbling within. "When I think of the pangs of conscience I've suffered over the way I've been harassing you, Jesse McPherson—and here you are, every bit as devious and conniving as I am."

"Yep. Looks as if we're two of a kind, all right."

Kali turned back to the suds with a small smile. She was startled to discover that she did feel a bond of sorts with Jesse...but one that had little to do with being devious or conniving. It was an elusive sort of feeling. In some way, because of straightforwardness and the appealing combination of grace and roughness that marked his movements, he reminded her of her brothers...of home. Yet there was a total absence of anything homey or brotherly in the way he'd been looking at her. She slanted a glance in his direction to verify that, and found him smiling at her, that undercurrent of sensual awareness in his look.

"Do you know you look really nice with your sleeves all scrunched up like that," he asked, "and with soapsuds on your nose?"

"I don't have soap—" Even as she denied it Kali swiped at her nose with the back of her hand.

"You do now." Jesse chortled.

"Why?" implored Kali, lifting her eyes to the ceiling. "With eight million people in this city, why do I have to be two of a kind with someone who has such a sick, adolescent sense of humor?"

"Just lucky, I guess."

"Or unlucky. Water seeks its own level, as my grandmother would say."

"No kidding? That's what mine would say, too. And as long as we're on the subject—"

"Of grandmothers?"

"No, of water. You've been soaking that pie plate—and your hands along with it—for what seems like hours. Now it's fine with me if you want to soak all day, but I have a nice big bathtub where we could both sit and be comfortable and..."

"And?" she prodded sassily when he trailed off with a suggestive gleam in his eye. Suggestive turned immediately to devilish, making Kali wish she'd remembered his ruthless streak before challenging him.

"And I think I'll save the rest for a surprise," he declared finally. "Maybe you'll be tempted by my air of mystery."

Chuckling, she lifted the plate from the rapidly cooling water and plopped it into his outstretched hand. "I do love solving a good mystery. Unfortunately, I've already done my quota of soaking for today." She twisted the plug at the bottom of the sink, sending the water swirling down the drain. "There, the dishes are done, kitchen's clean, and my stuff is all neatly packed up."

"That leaves only one job left to do," countered Jesse, taking a step closer to her. At Kali's puzzled frown, he continued, "Getting rid of those suds on your nose."

His hand stopped hers as she instinctively lifted it once more, and the look smoldering in his eyes froze her half-formed protest on her tongue. Tossing the dish towel over one shoulder, he circled the back of her neck with his warm, strong grip and tipped her face up to his. "The first step in the Jesse McPherson system of suds removal is for you to close your eyes."

Obeying the soft raspy command without a second thought, Kali let her eyelids drop, then caught her breath as the tip of his finger, warm and callused, tracked the trail of suds she still wasn't sure were really there. Not that she cared. At that moment her concerns began and ended with the gentle lingering pressure of his touch and the sweet yearning that sprang from deep within, spurring her pulse to a gallop and drawing her hands to his shoulders.

She felt the dampness of the towel resting beneath one hand, the solid curve of his shoulder beneath the other. It felt firm, toned, the muscles hinting at all the power and resiliency he had displayed on the ice. Only now it was the labyrinth of nerve endings along her neck and back that stirred beneath the magic persuasion of his touch.

The backs of his fingers glided across the ridge of her cheek; his mouth followed, moving in a moist, rambling path from her cheek to her closed eyelids...and finally to her lips. Inside her, heat waves surged and crested as he traced the full curve of her bottom lip with the tip of his tongue. He nipped playfully at the corners before drawing her into a kiss that was long and sweet and teasingly restrained.

His mustache swept across her cheek like a velvet brush as he moved to whisper close to her ear. "Kali, Kali, you smell so good."

The warm rush of his words sent goose bumps dancing over her skin, to be quickly followed by shivers as his tongue licked around and inside the delicate curve of her ear, flooding her and deafening her to all sounds, numbing her to all sensations but those he was arousing. It was a full moment before her muddled brain registered that he'd followed the husky compliment with an equally fervent "I must be crazy."

"No, you're not crazy," she whispered. "I do smell good. It's called Titiana, they gave me a whole case of it when I did an ad for—"

Jesse caged her face between his hands and lifted his head to smile down at her. It was not, Kali decided with a stab of anxiety, a happy sort of smile.

"Of course you smell good...you smell great. I didn't mean I was crazy because of what I was smelling, but because of what I was thinking...what I've been thinking ever since you walked in here."

"And what's that?"

"That I want to get to know you," he replied softly. The humor that had briefly touched his eyes was gone. "To spend time with you and find out if you really are as special as you seem to be."

"Is there something wrong with that?"

He shook his head, dropping his hands to his sides. "Not wrong, just crazy."

Kali watched him pace across the kitchen, his hands shoved in the back pockets of his worn jeans, emphasizing the solid width of his shoulders. Unbidden, a host of reasons why getting to know her wasn't in the least bit crazy ran desperately like ticker tape through her mind.

She bit her tongue on all of them. She'd done her share of pursuing—more than her share if she wanted to get picky about that. The ball was squarely in Jesse's court. If he wanted to play, he could damn well take his turn serving.

"My job is very demanding," he said abruptly, spinning back to face her. "I'm on the road a lot of the time, and even when I'm not, there are practices, public appearances. Then there's the pressure, like now with this winning streak—or worse, trying to get up for a game after a big loss. I can be a royal pain sometimes, and I need a woman who's able to put up with that."

"That doesn't seem like such a crazy thing to ask for."

"It would be crazy to ask it of you—you're just not that kind of woman."

Kali couldn't decide if the narrow line of his mouth expressed more disapproval or regret—and at that moment she couldn't have cared less. "How do you know what kind of woman I am?" she snapped. "You don't even know me."

"I know you're a model...and a very elite one at that, and—"

"Are we back to that again?" she interrupted in disbelief. "I thought we'd just spent the past couple of hours getting to know each other. Do you mean to tell me that I still seem to you like the kind of woman who's always on the make for a bigger fish to fry?"

A reluctant smile flitted across Jesse's mouth at the colorful expression. "No, you don't seem at all like what I expected you to be. What you seem like is every man's elusive dream woman...the perfect combination of beauty and brains and heart. Almost too good to be true. Unfortunately, I've learned that things that seem too good to be true usually are."

The trace of smile faded as he jerked his fingers through the dark waves of his hair. "But even if you were all you seem to be, it would still never work for us. I want a woman who's going to be there when I need her...who'll be around to put up with my moods. And you can save that outraged feminist look for the camera. I know your work is every bit as demanding and time-consuming as mine—that's the whole point. Can't you see that our jobs would always be pulling us apart? Instead of being there for each other, we'd only end up more frustrated, adding to each other's pressures, probably at each other's throats half the time."

"It wouldn't have to be like that," she ventured, trying to persuade him and at the same time wondering why she cared. "Sure, our seeing each other would involve juggling our free time and making some sacrifices—"

"I was never any good at making sacrifices," he interjected bluntly.

Kali exhaled through pursed lips, her nod slow and thoughtful. "I see. Then it would be crazy."

"Insane."

"You're absolutely right." Hooking her arm through the packed wicker basket on the counter beside her, she flashed him the full thousand-watt smile. "See you around."

Jesse proved to be as quick off skates as on. Maybe even quicker, thought Kali as he reached her before she got to the doorway and spun her around. He was satisfyingly stunned and thoroughly outraged.

"See you around?" he demanded, a scant decibel lower than the crash of thunder. "You can just turn and walk away from me with a cheerful little 'See you around'?"

"After the picture you painted, you're lucky I'm not running out of here screaming. Think of how that would look on the front page of tomorrow's sports section." She lowered her gaze pointedly to the spot where his fingers were clenched around her elbow. "And while you're at it, could you dispense with the caveman imitation? I bruise easily, and I'm doing a lay-out in a sleeveless gown first thing Monday morning."

He removed his hand as if she was on fire, but his scowl grew fiercer. "You see what I mean? We can't even argue because you have to pose in some fancy gown on Monday."

"We can argue all you want," she pointed out calmly, "I just won't allow you to manhandle me...not even if I was going to pose in a suit of armor on Monday."

His expression softened at the veiled accusation. "I don't want to manhandle you, Kali. Hell, I don't even want to argue with you. It's just that I can see all the problems and complications starting already."

"They're not starting, they're ending. See," she said, turning, "this is my back. Watch it go through your door. That means goodbye."

Jesse watched. He watched her cross his living room with the graceful, energetic stride that was hers alone. He watched her set the basket on the floor as she pulled on the red parka and zipped it, concealing beneath the plump layers of down the curves and hollows that haunted him nightly. He watched her retrieve her basket and head for the front door, ready to walk out of his apartment and his life without so much as a backward glance. He still couldn't believe she could actually do that, but this, he knew without a doubt, was not the time to sit around marveling at her spirit. Lurching from his position in the kitchen doorway, he was no longer an angry or a particularly philosophical man, simply a desperate one.

"Kali." To undermine his rapidly deflating ego, she didn't look the least bit surprised to hear the frantic edge to his voice. Turning slowly, she faced him with a faintly challenging expression in her beautiful blue eyes, making him wonder what on earth he was going to say next. Then, from out of nowhere, it came to him. "Will you have dinner with me tonight?"

Now she did look surprised—shocked, in fact. Probably, he thought with satisfaction, exactly the same way he'd looked when she had walked away with that flip little "See you around."

"You want to have dinner with me?" she demanded, "Even though it's obvious you have serious doubts about my character, probably wouldn't trust me as far as you could throw me, and think any involvement with me would be crazy?"

"I'd probably trust you as far I could throw you," he said slowly, as if that had been a tough decision—and was instantly rewarded with an intensifying of her exasperated expression.

"Thanks for nothing."

"Sorry—I couldn't resist. I do trust you, Kali. As for all the rest..." He trailed off with a shrug. "Do you want me to lie and tell you I have no doubts or concerns about whether we're good for each other, or do you want me to tell you the truth?"

Kali thrust her lower lip forward a teasing fraction of an inch while she mulled that over. It took every shred of his willpower to fight the instinct to lean closer and capture it between his own.

"I'm not sure which I would prefer," she admitted, just as a rush of pure, male instinct was about to best his self-control.

"Fine, we can talk about it some more over lunch." He lifted the basket from her hands and placed it on the floor just inside the front door.

"Lunch?"

He grinned. "Sure. Isn't that what usually comes after breakfast?"

"Not this soon after breakfast. We've only known each other a few hours, and so you've eaten one meal and made plans for two others. Can't you think of anything to do besides eat?"

Jesse didn't even try to curb the thoroughly delighted look her question inspired. "As a matter of fact, I can. But if we did *that* we wouldn't get much talking done. All things considered, I thought you'd probably prefer lunch."

"You're one hundred percent right," she assured him hastily. "And not just about lunch...about us being all wrong for each other, too."

A sensation that felt strangely like panic raced through Jesse at the thought that he might have gone too far, that this time she might really walk out. The fear was eased somewhat when he took a second, closer look at the sapphire eyes that sparkled teasingly up at him...eased but not erased completely, and Jesse didn't like the unfamiliar feeling of uncertainty one bit.

"Maybe neither one of us should jump to conclusions," he suggested in what he hoped sounded like an offhand manner. "After all, we don't really know enough about each other to decide for sure how we'll get along."

He watched Kali's slender shoulders lift in a careless shrug. She was annoyingly unswerved by his logic.

"I do know one very crucial thing," she countered. "Your job works pounds off and the camera adds them. No one would ever accuse me of being a diet fanatic, but given your obsession with eating, I'd say we fall into the category of professionally incompatible."

Jesse hid his sigh of relief in a long chuckle. "Is that all you're worried about?"

"It won't be funny if I can't zip up that gown come Monday morning."

"It will zip up because we're going to work off that breakfast before we have lunch."

"Work it off how?" Kali asked suspiciously, her hand tensing as he caught it in his, obviously ready to withdraw pronto if he should take a leading step in the wrong direction.

"Tsk-tsk. Not the way you're thinking," he admonished. "After all, technically this isn't even our first date. But there is an exercise room in the basement if you're interested."

Her head started shaking even before the last four words were out of his mouth. "No way—I hate to exercise."

"Thank God." He squeezed her hand. "I was afraid you might be the type who did leg lifts and sit-ups as a hobby."

Kali scrunched her lips as she frowned, managing somehow to tempt him with them even then. "When are you going to accept the fact that I am not any *type* at all?"

"Probably pretty soon now if you keep shattering all my illusions about models...but that still won't work off that breakfast." He paused, trying to think of something that might achieve the goal without countermanding his own aversion to exerting himself off the ice. Even more important, he had to keep Kali with him a while longer. All of a sudden that seemed to be his number-one goal in life. "I've got it. Do you like to walk?"

She smiled, and Jesse knew he had her.

"Great." He snatched his jacket from the spot behind the sofa where it had landed the night before and pulled it on.

"But I'm warning you," Kali said as he held the door open for her. "I like to walk at my own pace."

Hearing the determination in her voice, Jesse thought that was probably how Kali Spencer liked to do everything...at her own pace. The notion pleased him for some reason, and he was smiling broadly as he shot her a crisp salute. "Yes, ma'am, boss. I'll do my best to keep up."

They hadn't gone more than a block when Kali realized her warning had been unnecessary. Her feet and Jesse's rose and fell in perfect unison, their strides easy as they left his modern apartment building behind and strolled along the street lined with tenements and small neighborhood shops toward the park six blocks away.

Their conversation rolled along with the same easy rhythm. Small talk mostly, about things that had no real importance, but that were somehow devastatingly interesting because Kali and Jesse happened to be exchanging opinions on them. Kali scrupulously avoided the subject of her work, reluctant to test this new spirit of companionship and find that it might wither as quickly as it had bloomed.

Not that it mattered whether it bloomed or withered, some very practical part of her mind insisted on telling her. She couldn't deny that she was attracted to the man, but the timing was all wrong. For the past few months she'd been thinking more seriously than ever of retiring from modeling and moving back to North Dakota. The last thing she needed was to complicate an already difficult situation by getting involved with a man who had such strong professional ties to New York.

As she and Jesse skirted the small ice pond at the center of the park, a huge sheepdog streaked across their path, followed closely by a little girl with blond pigtails flying. Lurching to a halt to avoid falling flat on her face, Kali found herself rocking for balance against Jesse's solid frame. Instantly his arm was around her in a protective gesture that surprised her as much as the dog had. She looked up to see him smiling at her with bemused concern.

"I should have warned you," he said. "Traffic tends to get hazardous on these paths on Saturdays."

Kali nodded. "I'll say. I didn't even see those two coming."

"Neither did I," Jesse admitted, chuckling. "I'm just more used to reacting quickly on my feet than you are."

"Yeah, but that's on skates. I thought hockey players were supposed to have two left feet off the ice."

"I do. You haven't seen me dance yet."

"Yet?" Kali slanted a teasing glance up at him. "Is that an invitation?"

The corners of his dark mustache lifted with the full force of his grin. "Nope—a threat."

They started walking again, more slowly because his arm remained curled around her shoulders, even though she'd long since ceased needing it for balance. Or had she? Adrenaline was still pumping through her body, but activated now by feelings other than surprise or fear. For all the sparks his closeness sent shooting off inside her, she experienced an underlying sense of comfort at being nestled in the crook of Jesse's arm. She didn't feel she was about to be wrestled to the ground and devoured, as she had with a great many men she'd dated in the past five years.

From the very first she had no cause to fear Jesse's intentions. And for a very good reason, she thought with a bitter twist of amusement. Where she was concerned, he had none. She was, after all, not the kind of woman he wanted. Which was really too bad, because her emotional Geiger counter was sending off the signals that somewhere beneath his ruthless, often cynical facade might very well lurk exactly the kind of man *she* wanted.

"Are you going to share the joke or just go on walking around with that secret little smile?"

Jesse's gravel-edged drawl halted her musings. Share the joke? In this case, the answer was an unequivocal *no*.

Kali rapidly did a little creative embroidery on her thoughts and turned to meet his curious expression with a teasing grin. "Actually, I was thinking about what you said about your dancing. You sure don't move like a man who could threaten women with his technique."

"Really? What kind of man do I move like?"

Kali couldn't decide if it was his rough velvet tone or the slightly increased pressure of his arm around her that wove threads of sensual promise through the loaded question.

Exhaling the breath that had caught in her throat, she swept him with a studiously casual glance. "I'd say you move very deliberately, like a man who knows where he's going and how to get there. A man who knows what he wants and could dance circles around Fred Astaire, if that's what it took to get it."

She had meant the assessment to be light, teasing, but as the words came out, she knew she meant every one of them. When she faced Jesse's solemn gaze, she could tell he knew that, too.

"You make me sound so hard," he said quietly, stopping beside an ancient, gnarled maple that shielded them from the gusting December wind and the eyes of the other weekend strollers. "Do I really seem that hard to you, Kali?"

His fingers swept a few stray strands of silky blond hair from her cheek with unabashed tenderness, momentarily making the question sound absurd. But the intent look in his eyes reaffirmed all Kali's impressions of him and told her he would brook no answer but a totally honest one.

"You seem a little...stubborn, a little set in your ways."

"Why don't you just come right out and tell me I'm ornery and pigheaded?"

"All right, you're ornery and pigheaded. Does that make you feel better?"

"Not really." A self-deprecating smile gentled the hard line of his mouth. "If you'd asked me about this yesterday, I'd have told you I'm as hard as I have to be to get by. And that if people consider that being stubborn or ornery, that's their problem. But now..." His thoughtful gaze drifted over the crowded playground and the ball field, where a neighborhood football game was in full swing, before coming back to her. "Now, I don't want to be anything that will put that guarded, apprehensive look in your eyes."

"Well, how do you expect me to look when you threaten me with your dancing?"

Picking up on her attempt to lighten the mood, he smiled obligingly. "I guess I ought to just let you decide for yourself about my dancing...and about a lot of other things." He lifted her chin until she was staring directly into green eyes that were bright with passion and promises, but before she could untie her tongue to respond, he went on. "We'll start tonight...at least on the dancing part of it. Would you like to go dancing after we have dinner, princess?"

There was no sardonic shading to the nickname this time and Kali found herself smiling, "I haven't even agreed to have dinner with you yet."

Jesse slapped his open palm to his forehead in comic exasperation. "That's right—of course you haven't! Here I am planning the whole evening without your consent. I swear sometimes I have all the social grace of a baboon. I guess we'll just have to get our dinner plans straightened out over lunch."

While he was still rambling on, he started walking, cutting across to the far side of the park. Once more he settled his arm proprietorially around her shoulders and launched into a recitation of the entire menu of the small Greek restaurant where they were obviously headed. When he started on the desserts, Kali decided enough was enough. She interrupted with a sharp, two-fingered whistle she'd perfected years ago.

"Before you decide what to order for me," she began when she was sure she had his full attention, "I have a question—has anyone ever told you that you have a lot in common with a steamroller?"

"Just once." His mustache-tilting grin told her he wasn't surprised or offended by the comparison; he was immensely flattered. "A sports writer for the *Times* said I was like a steamroller on skates."

Kali's tawny brows arched. "Only on skates?"

"That's what the man said," Jesse countered with an ominous chuckle, "but then he'd never seen me dance, either."

4

"ALL RIGHT, KALI, what's the verdict?"

It was almost 11:00 P.M., and Kali was definitely beginning to feel weary after a day filled with the romance and excitement of Jesse McPherson. She had, of course, succumbed to his brash brand of charm and agreed to have dinner with him. In fact, they had returned to his place after lunch and become so enmeshed in a quarrelsome game of Trivial Pursuit that in the end she had succumbed again and accompanied him to his late-afternoon hockey practice in preparation for tomorrow's game. Afterward he drove her home and waited while she showered and changed for dinner.

The result was that they hadn't been out of each other's sight for more than a few moments all day, and Kali's reaction to his unadulterated male presence surprised her. It was true that his masculinity left her feeling overwhelmed, but not in the negative sense she was accustomed to. Jesse stirred her emotions in a way no other man ever had. With nothing more than a loaded glance or a whisper of a touch he could make her shimmer with sensations that were brand-new and seductive. Kali wondered if she would ever get enough...of the feeling or the man.

What was her verdict on his dancing, he had asked.

She smiled as they stepped off the elevator on the fourteenth floor and turned toward her corner apartment.

Valiantly she tried to come up with a tactful response. After dinner at an excellent but refreshingly untrendy Italian restaurant, they had stopped by a local club, where everything Jesse had threatened about his dancing had proved to be all too true.

"Hmm. A verdict," she mused. "Will you accept a simple guilty or not guilty?"

He took the key she pulled from her small, black leather purse and unlocked the door, then handed it back to her with a grin, thinking the old-world gesture might irk her. "That all depends on whether I'm found guilty or not guilty."

"Well, let's just say I definitely think you should forget what I said about your dancing circles around Fred Astaire—if that's what it would take to get something you wanted."

Jesse lifted one dark brow in an unmistakably challenging manner. "You think I'd just go without something I want?"

"Perish the thought." Kali's smile was slightly rueful. "But I can see now that it would be much more your style to simply knock the poor man down and grab what you wanted."

Jesse sighed and rested one shoulder against the hallway wall. "You're still annoyed because I told that guy at the club he couldn't dance with you."

"I'm not annoyed...even though what you told him was considerably more colorful than that."

His eyes narrowed. "I'm not sorry about it."

"Tell me something I can't see for myself," Kali shot back.

His careless, one-shouldered shrug held not a trace of remorse. "I said a lot of stupid things that first night we met, Kali, but one thing that I said I meant one hundred percent. I think if a lady is with a man she ought to stick with him and dance with him. *Only* him."

"Fine. I can buy that—even if it does have suspiciously prehistoric overtones. That doesn't excuse all the macho tripe about threatening to take the guy out back and teach him some manners."

"I did not threaten him," Jesse corrected calmly. "I simply pointed out that he had no manners. It was only after he asked what I planned to do about it that I suggested stepping outside. It seemed tidier than hurling him across the dance floor, which was my first impulse."

"I admit the guy was a little obnoxious—"

"He was a jerk."

"You still didn't have to respond to his stupid challenge. Couldn't you just have backed down and walked away?"

Jesse's eyes were lit with a curious combination of arrogance and amusement. "Not in this lifetime, honey."

"Oh, give me a break," groaned Kali. "*Honey?* That's almost as bad as calling me princess. No, on second thought I think it's worse."

He chuckled and straightened from the wall to loop his arms around her shoulders. "All right, you have my word—no more calling you honey. And fortunately that incident at the club didn't turn into a full-fledged scene...which saved you from being totally embarrassed and me from being slapped with an outrageous fine for brawling, courtesy of the hockey league. My public restraint also prevented a resurgence of my old nickname."

"Nickname?" echoed Kali, instantly intrigued by the disgruntled note in his voice.

"Yeah. Mount McPherson. Mount as in volcano," he added sheepishly in response to her quizzical expression. "Some aspiring comedian or a sports writer came up with it during my first pro season, back when I had a tendency to be a little...ah, volatile on the ice and off. Anyway, it stuck. Only during the past couple of seasons have I been able to shake it."

"Mount McPherson, huh?" Kali let her eyes sweep assessingly from his thick, dark hair to the leather boots he'd worn with his black suede jacket and gray corduroys.

Jesse responded to her smirk with a lazy smile and took a step closer. "That's right. How does it feel to date a volcano?"

At the moment, with his arms around her and his lean, muscled body brushing teasingly against her, he transmitted the same escalating excitement that probably did precede a volcano's eruption. And he felt wonderful. But that was the last thing she was going to admit to a man who still had done little more than give in gracefully to her advances, and who could look so irritatingly smug at times. Such as right now, for instance.

"All things considered," she announced decisively, "I think I would have chosen a different nickname for you. Something more evocative of the real you. Something like—" she fought back a grin as she met his increasingly wary gaze "—Caveman McPherson. That's it, Caveman. It's perfect."

"Caveman?" His mustache twisted above a half smile.

Kali nodded enthusiastically. "Right. I detected evidence of it right away. You have very obvious and pronounced Neanderthal tendencies...in spite of all your superficial attempts to appear civilized." She gave his silk tie a yank. "Tell the truth now—deep down don't you feel more like a caveman than a volcano?"

His half smile evolved into a tantalizingly wicked grin. Sliding one hand up from her shoulder, he wound her hair tightly around it in a gesture straight from another, earlier age and used the hold to tip her face up to his.

"Now that you mention it, I do sometimes feel as if there's this alter ego inside trying to get out...someone not nearly as polished and charming as I am." He chuckled, and the low-pitched sound slithered over Kali like raw silk, every bit as seductive as the touch of his lips on the side of her throat. "He seems especially restless tonight," he continued in a whisper, his breath a rush of moist heat against her skin. "What do you say, Kali? Want to help me indulge my fantasy a little?"

Kali's breath caught at the sudden hunger in his soft voice, but she didn't push him away, and she didn't utter the unequivocal no that her instincts for self-preservation told her to. Instead she allowed him to pull her a little closer to the fire in him, and she smiled as her eyelids drifted shut. She had no intention of indulging any of his fantasies...at least not on their first date. But she had been crazily tempted all night to explore a little further the magic that had seemed to sizzle between them in his kitchen that morning. The female desires clamoring inside told her this was her chance.

Of course what she *thought* she'd felt in his arms could not possibly be real, she'd been telling herself repeatedly and to absolutely no avail. Of course the earthshaking feeling of being consumed by fire couldn't actually happen. At least it didn't happen overnight to a twenty-five-year-old woman who had dated a healthy cross section of the male population and had never felt anything more than a pleasant but easily controlled response to any man's kiss or touch.

Still, when Jesse had held her in his arms as they danced, she been overwhelmingly aware of the supple power in him and could think of nothing but the way the taut muscles of his back and shoulders had felt that morning as they flexed in response to her caressing fingers. And each time his mustache tilted in humor, she could almost feel it brushing roughly across her cheek, stirring up that unfamiliar swirling sensation in the pit of her stomach. In all probability, her response to him had been due more to frayed nerves than magic, but she wouldn't sleep tonight unless she found out for sure.

Without waiting for her to accept or reject the invitation to share his fantasy, Jesse abandoned the trail of damp kisses he was stringing along the slant of her jaw and brought his mouth to hers. His touch was light at first as he used the barest tip of his tongue to paint her lips with his own moistness, then urged them fully apart to allow him entrance. The kiss deepened rapidly and provocatively, with long, deep strokes that grated his tongue roughly against hers and brought Kali's hands up to seek the support of his broad shoulders. His touch had set the world spinning. His fingers slipped from her hair to her waist to pull her closer, closer, until their bodies were melded from shoulder to knee and Kali wasn't sure if the hard pounding she felt against her rib cage was from her heart or his.

Hazily she registered that she had the answer to her question. What she felt in Jesse's arms was indeed magic, not simply an attack of nerves that could be conveniently explained away. The roughness of his mustache and the soft warmth of his lips teased and aroused her as he moved with tantalizing slowness to an excruciatingly sensitive spot on her neck. As Kali's whole body arched in response, she knew Jesse was able to make her feel something else, as well—something as powerful as magic and up until now just as scarce in her life—raw passion. The thought alarmed even as it excited her, but at that moment Kali's mind was too scrambled to dwell on what her responses *should* have been. She only knew what existed—a furious sensual burning she could neither halt nor control...and didn't want to.

When his lips claimed hers demandingly once more, Kali felt the buttons along the front of her coat being freed one by one. Then it was tugged open, and Jesse's hand slipped inside, his touch warm and gentle on the skin at the V-neckline of her silk blouse. His fingers easily found a path beneath the loose fabric to brush across the tip of her breast. It hardened in a revealingly eager response, and Kali felt a melting rush—as if some previously untested dam inside had given way, releasing a torrent of pure longing. Her own muffled groan echoed Jesse's as he abruptly yet reluctantly broke the kiss and used both arms to pull her close to his chest.

"Oh, Kali, I want to come inside with you tonight...now."

Somehow Kali rallied enough of her scattered control to bite back an impulsive agreement, reminding herself just how dangerous it might be to have Jesse in her apartment. She detested the after-date-coffee-and-grope-on-the-sofa routine. Although this time, she had to admit, the danger lay much more in her own precarious ability to resist Jesse's advances. No. If for no other reason than to avoid confirming his opinion that all models were easy and sleazy, she was not letting him in.

Pressing her palms against his chest in an unconscious prelude to her refusal, she lifted her eyes to find his filled with passion, glimmering like polished jade. "Jesse, I'm sorry, but—"

"Shh." His fingertip touched her lips, bringing her words to a quavery halt. "Before you go putting flimsy excuses between us, let me finish. I *want* to come in with you tonight, but I can't. We have a game tomorrow afternoon, and I've learned the hard way that my tired old body isn't up to par after a long, sleepless night." As he spoke, his thumb coasted over her cheek with a gentleness that was strangely at odds with the longing in his eyes. "And although no night with you could ever be long enough to suit me, I can promise you our first night together will be very sleepless."

Kali flushed at the blunt promise, feeling disappointment instead of relief twisting through her. She was suddenly very aware of the rise and fall of his chest beneath her hands, and she let them fall awkwardly to her sides as she searched for something casual to say.

"Well," she ventured finally, "I hardly think being thirty relegates your body to the ranks of the old and tired."

Jesse's lips tilted in a slightly self-deprecating grin. "It does if you've spent over half those years being slammed into the boards of an ice rink and having high-flying pucks ricochet off your back."

Kali frowned, recalling the violent skirmishes of the other evening's game with new concern, now that one of the men being slammed and pounded was Jesse.

"I've always known hockey was rough, even the high-school and college varieties my brothers played. But pro hockey is even more—" she couldn't suppress a sudden shiver "—intense. Why would a man who's garnered all sorts of awards and most-valuable-player trophies—not to mention an assortment of broken bones and pulled muscles—go on playing year after year?"

"Why, Kali, it sounds as if you've been doing a little personal research, too." His smile teased her but he proceeded graciously after her embarrassed shrug. "As for why I go on playing...just for the thrill of it, I guess. I don't expect you to understand that...my own mother doesn't, despite all the times I've tried to explain it to her. But I get a rush from facing off against another player and coming out on top that I just don't think I'd get from selling used cars or working in the family restaurant. I need that rush."

"It compensates for all the aches and pains?"

Jesse shrugged. "More or less. Besides, when I do retire, I want to go out a winner, and that means the Stanley Cup. The Bandits have a shot at winning it this season...but not if I sleepwalk through a big game like the one tomorrow...even if the reason is blond and beautiful, with skin softer than anything I've ever touched."

He punctuated the husky words with kisses and strokes along her throat that made Kali's world tilt and blur. "It's a new skin cream," she offered distractedly. "Velvet Touch. I—"

"I know," he interrupted, his gritty chuckle a different sort of caress. "They gave you a whole case when you did an ad for it. Will you put some on again tomorrow when you come to watch me play?" Eyes gleaming wickedly, he added, "My contract doesn't say anything about the way I spend the night after a big game."

It was clear to Kali that he was offering her much more than a free ticket to a hockey game. "Your job might not be a problem," she said regretfully, "but I'm afraid mine will be. I have to be on location bright and early Monday morning. *Very* early," she emphasized before he had a chance to comment.

Undaunted, Jesse replied, "All right, but you can still come to the game, can't you?"

Yielding to her own desire to see him play again, Kali smiled broadly. "Why not? After all, it's not every day I get a personal invitation from old Mount McPherson himself."

THE CROWD THAT streamed from the Colosseum early the following evening was considerably less exuberant than the group that had cheered the players on after the first game Kali had attended. And with good reason. The Bandits had fallen behind early in the second period, then had their winning streak snapped in an agonizing rout. Although it would be stretching the point to say Jesse was responsible for his team's defeat, undoubtedly his performance lacked the finely honed moves and split-second reactions that had made him famous.

Kali watched him play with mounting concern. With an ease that belied their short acquaintance, she could read the frustration and impatience in the lines of his body. She held her breath in dread each time a spectator shouted an explicit opinion about his talent...or lack thereof. Jesse ignored the gibes and conserved his energy for scuffling with the players on the opposing team. There were several outbursts, especially toward the end of the game as time and tempers grew short, and Kali cringed whenever Jesse was involved in an episode of violent high-sticking, whether he was on the giving or receiving end of the action.

It wasn't until the final buzzer sounded that she admitted the truth to herself. The giant knot in her stomach resulted from more than her concern that Jesse's temper might catapult him into the stands to silence a mouthy fan. From the instant the Bandits had skated onto the ice, she had been heartwrenchingly aware of a detail that had barely caught her interest during the last game. Jesse McPherson was one of only two Bandits, and one of only a handful of players in the entire league, who played without a helmet. In a game where brute force turned the puck into a hundred-mile-an-hour missile, refusing to wear a helmet seemed to Kali a foolish and unnecessary risk to take. Her fear for Jesse confirmed that she felt more than lust for him.

Jesse's face was an icy mask as he stepped from the rink to the ramp leading to the locker room. This time there was no bantering with the fans and not even a glance toward where Kali sat in the section reserved for friends and families of the team. The hard expression shaping his chiseled features lent an ominous reality to the nickname they had joked about the previous night. Kali made her way to the agreed-upon spot outside the team exit, not knowing whether the easygoing Jesse she'd shared breakfast with or an explosive caveman would finally emerge.

Inside the locker room, Jesse slung his gym bag over his shoulder and headed for the exit. He knew he'd kept Kali waiting longer than he should have, and he knew that each delaying moment was absolutely essential if he was to face her with anything resembling control over his emotions. No doubt he would be raked over the coals royally in the morning sports pages, but nothing written there could equal the abuse he would heap on himself for some time to come. What a miserable performance! Others might call it a fluke, the result of burnout or simply an off day, but he knew what he had been was *distracted*. Today, more than ever, he had wanted to be dazzling in his moves, to impress Kali with his finesse, and he'd blown it. Hell, she was the reason he'd blown it. He knew that even if no one else did.

Slamming his hand against the push bar on the door, he muttered an expressive oath. He had no one to blame but himself for screwing up out there tonight. He'd known from the start that Kali Spencer was going to wreak havoc with his concentration. He should have had the sense to resist the challenge she presented, to stick to the kind of women who proved safe in the past—those who were easy conquests or just plain easy.

Stepping from the steam-heated building into the cold of approaching winter, he found Kali waiting where he'd told her to. Her hands were thrust deep into the pockets of her red jacket, and her collar was turned up as an ineffectual shield for cheeks that were already pink and wind whipped. Jesse took one look at her standing alone and damned himself again...this time for keeping her waiting out in the cold while he licked his wounds.

Crossing the nearly empty parking lot with long strides, he came close to her and framed her face with his hands. He frowned. "God, Kali, you're frozen. You should have waited in the car."

"Really? I was wondering if maybe I should have just hopped a bus instead."

Jesse hated seeing wariness in the deep blue eyes that were usually warm and bright when she looked at him. "I'm sorry I took so long."

"It wasn't that," she explained hurriedly. "I just wasn't sure what sort of mood you'd be in after..."

He watched her search for a gentle way to say it and felt a sudden burning need to make things easy for her...always. If it killed him, he wasn't going to take his frustration out on her.

Forcing as much of a smile as he could, he prompted, "You mean after my being totally humiliated in front of thousands of people? Let's just say I started at acute self-loathing and went downhill rapidly."

"Jesse, it wasn't your fault—"

"Kali, don't. I know what role I played in tonight's fiasco, and while I appreciate your support, it really doesn't change the only thing that counts—the final score. So let's just forget about it, okay?"

She eyed him with blatant skepticism. "Do you really think you can forget it?"

This time his smile came a little easier. "I think I might manage...with a whole lot of help from you."

She didn't answer, simply smiled back in that half shy, half sexy way that kept him awake nights, and Jesse was suddenly in a hurry to get someplace warm and cozy. With one arm holding her close to his side, he started walking toward his car.

"Hey, Jesse...wait up."

The unmistakable bellow of his friend and teammate Gary Reardon stopped him just as he was swinging open the passenger door of his low-slung black Jaguar. The other man hustled across the lot to join them, rubbing his gloveless hands briskly.

"Man, it is colder than a witch's—" He broke off with a sheepish glance in Kali's direction. "Well, it's just pretty cold out here."

"Kali, this is Gary. Gary, Kali Spencer."

His teammate's eyes flashed with recognition at Jesse's brief introduction. "Kali...Jesse's Ice Princess. I'll bet you feel right at home in this weather, huh?"

Kali returned his friendly smile. "Actually, at the moment I think I'm frozen past the point of feeling anything."

"I'm sorry," Gary said instantly. "I won't keep you standing here talking. I just wanted to tell Jesse that some of the guys are coming back to my place for a few beers—sort of a drown-your-sorrows party. You're welcome, too, Kali."

Jesse shook his head. "I don't think so, Gary. I don't feel much like doing any kind of partying tonight."

"I've got some news that might cheer you up. I just heard from some guy who was in the Raiders' locker room after the game that you loosened two of Orwing's front teeth when you two clashed in the last period. He's probably going to lose them."

"That's real tough."

Kali jerked around to face Jesse, struck by the thread of utter contempt running through his gravel voice. "Who's Orwing?"

"Just about the dirtiest player in the league," Jesse told her. "If I'd known we were going to lose, anyway, I would have said to hell with the penalty and knocked all his teeth out."

The careless way he uttered the violent threat and the cold sheen in his eyes haunted Kali as they said good-night to Gary and climbed into the car. As he whipped the high-performance vehicle around corners with daredevil speed and wove an aggressive path between other cars on the congested city streets, she tried telling herself that he was simply working out his frustration...feeling the same way she felt when she'd thought she'd blown a big assignment. The thought didn't lessen her uneasiness. Especially when he seemed to slip from simply untalkative into black silence by the time they reached her apartment.

Kali had fallen in love with the apartment the instant she'd seen the living room and had signed the lease on the spot, even before she could technically afford the exorbitant rent. The room was designed so that the huge windows of both outside walls met in the corner, presenting a nearly panoramic view of the city. She had decorated in shades of pewter and rose, aiming for a sleek, sophisticated look. The effect, Kali acknowledged cheerfully, was sabotaged by the abundance of framed family photographs all around and the brightly striped afghan—a birthday present from her grandmother—that lay across the back of an old pine rocker from home.

Jesse appeared to notice none of it. While she hung up their coats, he paced restlessly, finally pausing to stare out the night-blackened windows with a bitter expression that told Kali he was seeing only his own private reruns of the game. He responded eagerly when she asked if he'd mind starting a fire in the white marble fireplace, obviously grateful for any distraction from his own thoughts. Leaving him to fiddle with logs and kindling, Kali headed for the kitchen to make hot chocolate and arrange an assortment of cheese and crackers on a tray. She returned a few minutes later to find the fire blazing and Jesse sitting on the sofa before it. Brooding. There was no other word to describe his mood, and Kali began to wonder what real "help" she could be to Jesse at that moment.

"Dig in," she urged, lowering the tray to the glass-topped coffee table and sitting beside him on the sofa.

Jesse reached for the steaming mug closest to him and took a cautious sip, then surprised her by permitting a reluctant smile to soften his mouth. "Hot chocolate?"

Kali nodded. "I figured the last thing your nerves needed tonight was a shot of caffeine."

"Why? Do I seem jittery to you?"

She shook her head at his defensive tone. "No, but I know you're upset, and I thought this might help relax you."

"Thanks," he said with a shrug so weary it caught at Kali's heartstrings.

"If you want the truth—" she placed a hand lightly on his arm "—what you really seem is exhausted. You should probably just go to bed."

"Is that an invitation?"

"Not unless you fancy stretching your six-foot body out on my five-foot sofa."

"I can think of places I'd much rather stretch my body out."

"Drink your hot chocolate," ordered Kali, more affected by his suggestive growl than she cared to reveal. "It's getting late."

"On the other side of the world, maybe. Here on the east coast it's not even nine o'clock."

His hand moved caressingly over her back, imparting a sweet, soft thrill that was a potent challenge to her self-control. "Yes, but tomorrow *I* happen to have a big game."

A slow smile creased Jesse's face. "I didn't even know you played."

"I don't—it's called work. Remember the gown layout I told you about yesterday?" She didn't wait for a reply. "Well, it's scheduled for sunrise."

There was a loud clunk as he lowered his mug to the table and snapped, "That's just perfect. I guess I should just shove off, then."

Anger flashed through Kali. "I guess maybe you should. It seems as if you'd rather be alone, anyway."

"Not at all—I'd rather be with my woman."

"Really? Is she anyone I know?"

"Don't play games with me, Kali."

"What do you expect?" She flounced back to the far corner of the sofa, arms crossed protectively in front of her. "This may come as a big shock to you, Caveman, but I don't like being referred to as 'my woman,' especially when we've only known each other a grand total of two days."

"It doesn't feel as if we've only known each other two days."

Kali shrugged, avoiding his searching gaze, but she couldn't avoid the truth in his quiet assertion. "I don't care how it feels," she lied. "That's the way it is."

"Kali." It was a stark, one-word challenge.

She raised her eyes slowly and was shocked by the perception she saw in his blatantly mocking expression. "Oh, all right. Maybe it does feel as if we've known each other a little longer than that—"

"A lot longer."

"Okay—a lot longer. And I know you're feeling lousy about losing that game, and I wish I could help, but I'm not going to bed with you just to cheer you up, even if I didn't have an early shoot tomorrow. I'm just not ready."

His expression gentled at the defiance in her voice. "You're right, Princess. Believe me—despite all my crass hinting—I'm not trying to steamroll you into bed. I don't want it to happen until you are ready...until you want it as much as I do...if it's humanly possible for anyone else to want someone as much as I want you," he added dryly.

Kali lowered her eyes to the plush, steel-toned carpet, flattered by his remark and more than a little aroused by the sensual promise in the dark eyes she could still feel sliding over her.

"I think I want you already, Jesse," she revealed softly. "But I have to be sure. In spite of all you've seen and heard about models, there haven't been a lot of men in my life...not that way."

"I know that, Kali." His deep voice was underscored with a certainty that filled her with relief. "And I want you to know something. When I got angry a few minutes ago it wasn't because you shot me down before I even got started...it was your reason for doing it."

She sighed, knowing the answer even before she asked the question. "Because of my job?"

"Right. I know it's crazy, and I have no right to expect you to let me interfere with your work...but I do expect that." He smiled, a sheepish, half-crooked smile that touched someplace deep inside Kali with wonder and sapped any resentment she might have felt. "I just wanted to be with you tonight, and when you said you couldn't because of some sunrise 'shoot,' it just brought back into focus all the reasons I know it will never work with us."

"All the reasons you regaled me with yesterday?"

"And then some. Never mind the fact that you'll probably never be around at the times I need you most...I hadn't even considered the mess you're going to make of my game."

"Me?" Kali demanded incredulously.

"You're damn right you," he fairly bellowed. "Like today for instance—I've never, ever missed a slapshot from ten feet before."

"I can't believe you're actually trying to pin the blame on me for what happened out there today."

"Well, you're the one who distracted me—who should I blame?" His tongue was in his cheek now; his mood was improving by the minute.

"You said it yourself—you *are* getting older."

"That has nothing to do with it."

"And neither did I."

"You want to bet?"

"Why?" she demanded, waving her arm excitedly and trying to ignore the infuriating grin that was working its way across his face. "Just so you can prove me wrong? So I can listen to you gripe every time I'm too busy to pat your back and say, 'Poor Baby'? There are only two reasons things will never work out for us—and that's because you're so all-out determined to fight every step of the way. And because you want your *own* way. Well, as far as I'm concerned you can stop fighting."

Jesse deflected the pillow she hurled in the general direction of his twitching mustache, inquiring casually, "Is this by any chance another surrender?"

"Not by a long shot," snapped Kali. "In fact I just decided there's no way I want to get involved with a man who's always pounding on his chest like some throwback from prehistoric times.

As her temper flared she had leaned forward, making it simple for Jesse to snare her wrists and tumble her across his lap, adding a very interesting emphasis to his silky words. "You haven't been paying attention, Kali, love. We already *are* involved."

5

FINALLY KALI CONVINCED Jesse that she wasn't going to change her mind, that she really did have to be up before the sun and that he really did have to leave. Her task had been expanded to heroic proportions by her body's mutinous response to his hungry kisses and exploring caresses. Even when he'd gone, the good night's sleep she so sorely needed was held at bay by thoughts of him.

She tried a warm bath, a boring book, a cup of herbal tea, but none of the tried-and-true methods were relaxing enough to plummet her into sleep, or to chase away the image of the raven-haired, jade-eyed man whose smile could make her forget her own name.

While she lay in bed, bits and pieces of what they'd said to each other filtered through her mind. She recalled all his cynical arguments why they would never be able to get along, and her own compelling urge to convince him otherwise. She shivered beneath the layers of blankets as her parade of disjointed thoughts fused into the clarity of Jesse's fiery gaze and dauntless tone. He was right. Discussing the wisdom of becoming involved was pointless, because they already were.

Obviously, thought Kali, rolling onto her stomach, her powers of persuasion were even greater than she'd thought, but she wondered if maybe she hadn't been wrong, after all. Oh, she was sure they could work out the logistics of dating each other. Years of coping with the photographers' penchant for shooting at sunrise and sunset had rendered her adept at making the most of whatever part of the day was left to her. Their dating schedule might not be strictly conventional. What bothered her—and what she was having trouble making the romantic free spirit inside her pay attention to—was her increasingly strong suspicion that Jesse McPherson was not the sort of man who belonged in her future.

Her dreams hadn't changed a whole lot in the five years since fate had sent out a scout for a New York modeling agency. The scout had toured the state university where Kali was studying to become a special-education teacher. To Kali, who was accustomed to her brothers' reluctant admission that she was "all right looking...but skinny," the scout's pronouncement that she had great bones and fantastically alluring eyes was as irresistible a call as the Pied Piper's tune. She would have eagerly followed that woman much farther than New York.

When she had first arrived in the city, she had been overwhelmed by the glamour and excitement that sizzled there twenty-four hours a day. Gloria, the agency's resident mother hen, had consoled a nervous, slightly homesick Kali by assuring her that in no time this would all seem more routine and less awesome, and she would get into the full social swing. Gloria had been right on one count. It hadn't taken long for whatever enchantment the endless round of glitzy parties had held for Kali to wear off. As her career skyrocketed, her interest in all the perks that went with success dwindled. She became a dropout from the social circuit even before she'd become a full-fledged member.

The lack of contact with other models limited her circle of close friends to Glen and a few others she'd met through her volunteer work, but that didn't bother her. Despite her affection for Glen and the others, when she thought of friends she thought of home—Williston and the friendships she'd nurtured since grade school. And she thought of Rick Logan, the boyfriend she'd left behind when she had come to New York to seek fame and fortune. Well, now she had more fame and fortune than she had ever wanted, and her best friend, Rebecca Blackwell, had Rick Logan.

It wasn't really because of Rick that Kali felt a twist of longing whenever she thought about Rebecca. She was realistic enough to know that she and Rick probably would have drifted apart even if she'd stayed home. But those other things that Rebecca had—and she didn't— filled her with restlessness. Things like a real home instead of a silent, empty apartment to return to at the end of the day, a husband and children of her own and a job at the local nursery school, which demanded more of Rebecca than great bone structure and some acting ability.

All those things figured prominently in Kali's dreams for the future. She wanted all the little, ordinary things most people took for granted...like living close enough so that she could attend family birthday parties and have her nieces and nephews ride their bikes over to visit after school. After five years of missing the small town she had once considered hokey, Kali wanted to go home. And that was why letting herself become more than casually involved with Jesse McPherson would be as foolhardy as playing with dynamite.

From what she'd seen so far of his combination of temperament and charm, Jesse had a lot in common with dynamite. He had said himself that he craved the rush of excitement, needed the thrill of taking a risk, and Kali had suspected from the start that those needs applied to his life off ice as well as on. Releasing a sigh into the soft down pillow, she admitted that maybe he wasn't as different from the other men she'd dated as his offhand manner and faded denims had first suggested. He might be seeking a different sort of thrill than high-powered attorneys and corporation presidents were, and using a different style of power play to get it, but the effect was the same.

From his helmetless style of play to the ruthless way he could dismiss an opponent's injury or bully another man in a bar, Jesse was a risk taker. Not at all the sort of man to be content sitting on a front-porch swing in a town like Williston. He wouldn't be any happier there, sharing her dreams, than she would be staying in the city and watching him play until he was too old to take the grueling physical punishment, then "retiring" to something just as competitive and demanding of his time, like coaching or sportscasting.

Whatever he finally deemed thrilling and exciting enough to hold his interest after hockey, Kali was certain he wouldn't find it in Williston, as certain as she was that she was going home. She didn't know exactly when, but she wanted to leave while she was still riding high in her career and eager to tackle whatever the future held, not with a broken heart and anguished second thoughts to haunt her for the rest of her life.

It was, she instructed herself with a yawn, something she must keep in mind at all times when dealing with Jesse. And yet, as sleep at last tugged at her eyelids and misted her thoughts, she was filled with a delicious feeling of anticipation...a feeling that was totally inappropriate for a woman on the brink of becoming involved with the wrong man.

JESSE BIT DOWN hard on his bottom lip and tried to concentrate on the scarred plaster of the locker room wall, not on the wrenching pain in his knee.

"You pulled the muscle all right, Jess," the team trainer finally announced. "Pulled it good this time."

"No kidding," Jesse growled, glaring over his shoulder at the rugged, middle-aged man who'd been poking and stretching his damaged left leg for what felt like hours. "How long?"

He twisted to sit up on the examining table, feeling in his creaking bones and throbbing left knee the cumulative effect of years of pushing his body to the limit.

Joe, the trainer, tossed him a towel and eyed him critically. "How long? That's hard to say."

Jesse held his breath as he waited for the official decision. How long was the stupid mistake he'd made during this morning's practice going to sideline him?

"Now if you was the type of guy to do as I say," continued Joe in the friendly, sparring manner the two had developed through years of working together, "like spending an hour in the whirlpool and staying off that leg the rest of the day, then I'd say with tape and cortisone you might—*might*—be back in business for the game on Thursday. But being the kind of know-it-all you are—"

"All right, all right, you old witch doctor." Jesse's disgusted tone was punctuated by a painful wince as he slid off the table, bringing his weight down on his injured leg. "I'll play it your way this time."

Joe hurriedly extended a helping hand as Jesse headed for the whirlpool, shaking his head disapprovingly when his hand was impatiently swept aside. "Play it my way, he says. Ha! I'll believe that when I see it. You don't even know enough to keep your weight off it while I'm still watching you."

"So who asked you to watch me?"

The barbed exchange went on as Jesse shucked the rest of his practice uniform and carefully lowered himself into the whirlpool, the bickering ending only when Joe was called away to see to another player. In the silence that followed, Jesse found the soft, bubbling sound of the water soothing. The swirling warmth around his leg eased the discomfort considerably, leaving him free to concentrate on other things, mostly on the thing he shouldn't be concentrating on at all...Kali. Mooning over how warm and soft she'd felt last night in his arms, he'd missed that pass from Gary, then lunged for it too late and wound up twisting the same knee the doctor had told him to favor if he wanted to last through this season. His *last* season, he reminded himself, black brows lowering over an expression that was both angry and regretful.

It had come as no surprise when the bone specialist informed Jesse he wouldn't be able to play past this season without an operation on his knee. The knee had been plaguing him off and on since college, but Jessie had long ago decided that the complicated operation, with its fifty percent chance of success, was not for him. Hell, he'd never wanted to play hockey forever, anyway, and he was damn sick of all the time on the road. How he wanted to go out a winner. Winning the Stanley Cup would take all the sting out of being forced to retire because of his knee.

That was the reason he hadn't told anyone, not his family or friends or the team brass, about his decision. He would win first and make his announcement later. He had it all planned perfectly. At least, he'd had it all planned perfectly until Kali had strolled into his life and proceeded to upset applecarts all over the place. She was all he thought about, and these days he couldn't afford to be that mesmerized by anything but a hockey puck. If the

Bandits were going to take the championship, they needed him...all of him, not just the mangled scraps that would be left behind if Kali turned out to be as self-centered and dangerous as everything in his past experience told him a woman that beautiful had to be. She might have been born in a small town, but she'd come a long way since then, and graced a lot of magazine covers, and probably developed a lot of bad habits he just hadn't gotten close enough yet to see.

Resting his head on the curved edge of the tub, Jesse thought he might just have hit on the solution to his problem. Instead of fighting his obsession, maybe he should feed it. Familiarity with Kali might not breed contempt, but it sure might reveal enough flaws to break this embarrassingly adolescent fascination he felt for her. He flexed his left leg gingerly, testing the suppleness of the knee joint. It felt better already, and so did he now that he'd decided on a new plan of action. After Kali, he planned to get on with the rest of his life.

Straightening in the tub, he glanced at the clock on the opposite wall. He'd been soaking for fifty-two minutes. Not quite the hour Joe had ordered, he acknowledged as he hoisted himself out, but it was all the time he could spare if he was going to reach the downtown office of the Prestige Modeling Agency before the secretary left for lunch. After all, he wouldn't be able to bribe information out of someone who wasn't there.

An hour later, Muriel Connors was thrilled to have in her possession two tickets to the next Bandits home game, and Jesse was on his way to Greenacres Park on Fifty-first Street, where Kali was shooting the evening-gown layout for *Vogue.* By narrowly avoiding the rear bumpers of several taxis and driving with two wheels on the curb for a short stretch on Second Avenue, he made the drive

through heavy traffic in record time. As he lurched to a
stop across from the small park, he heaved a sigh of relief
to see barricades still in place to keep onlookers back. Ignoring the No Parking sign, Jesse limped from the car,
shouldered his way to the front of the crowd of gawkers
and froze.

The scene had been carefully orchestrated so that the
quaint, almost nostaligic background contrasted with the
sleek contemporary gowns being featured in the photo
spread. On an ivy-covered wall in front of the waterfall sat
a model about ten years old, wearing pigtails, jeans and a
look of wide-eyed wonder as she stared at Kali. Jesse stared
at Kali, too—gaped, in fact—but his wide-eyed look was
genuine, with definite glints of masculine hunger mixed
in. Masculine and hungry was exactly how he felt as he
watched Kali move in a gown that was no more than a
crimson flame of silk that left one shoulder enticingly bare
and flowed over her slender body with teasing sensuality.

With great effort he tore his eyes from her and scanned
the crowd around him. Most of the other men there looked
a little on the hungry side, too, and for some reason that
bothered Jesse to no end. It also bothered him that he was
already shivering inside his leather jacket, while Kali was
standing out there in a hell of a lot less. Didn't that wimpy-
looking photographer realize it was only forty-eight degrees out today? Probably not, he decided with a sardonic twist of his lips as he noted the photographer's heavy
jacket, plaid scarf and woolen beret.

He turned back to stare at Kali, remembering how he'd
spent the whole ride in from Long Island coaching himself on the most prudent way to handle his new approach
toward her. He would see her as much as his schedule per-
mitted, but at the same time he would be sensible. He had
confidently assured himself that he would keep his eyes

open and his guard up, and get out before he got in too deep. Now as he drank in the sight of her, he realized he'd wasted his time plotting a strategy. Prudent and sensible just didn't mesh with the hot, hungry way she made him feel.

The soft fabric of the gown clung to her thighs as she swirled and posed, and Jesse remembered how those long legs had felt pressed against him last night. His eyes caressed the silk-covered curve of her breasts, and his palm burned to touch her there again. His gaze wandered over her shoulders, the dip of her waist, the pleasing roundness of her hips, and in that instant Jesse knew he wanted Kali Spencer and he meant to have her. . .the consequences be damned. He also knew he didn't like watching her freeze her butt off while a bunch of business types spent their lunch hour leering.

"Nice, Kali, love. Now a hint of a smile. . .sultry. . .no teeth."

The photographer's nasal voice drifted back to Jesse, fueling his distaste for the whole scene. He squinted, trying to discern traces of discomfort in Kali's obligingly sultry smile. He wished he could get close enough to see if she had goose bumps on her arms. Hell, she had to have goose bumps—it was freezing out here. Even his leg was beginning to throb again.

"That's wonderful, love," the photographer cooed in a tone Jesse found distinctly nauseating. "Miranda, keep your eyes on Kali, sweetie. . .and keep looking enchanted."

The kid could afford to look enchanted, thought Jesse. *She* was wearing a heavy sweater. His narrowed eyes detected a slight shiver as Kali tossed back her hair to expose the star-shaped cluster of diamonds adorning each ear. He had to stuff his hands in his jacket pockets to keep from vaulting over the barricade, grabbing the coat being held by an assistant on the sidelines and bundling it around her.

"More excitement, Kali," the photographer urged. "Remember, love, you're supposed to be dressed for the evening of your life...on your way to meet a very special man. Think sultry...think steam."

The unfortunate choice of words was all Jesse needed to tip him over the edge. With a quick, none-too-graceful move that sent pain knifing through his whole left side, he was over the barricade. "How the hell do you expect her to think steam when she's freezing to death, for God's sake?" he demanded of the startled photographer.

Kali felt neither cold nor hot as she watched Jesse stumble past Stan Osenheimer, one of the top fashion photographers in the country, and grab her black wool coat from his assistant. She felt numb—the embarrassed, disbelieving variety of numbness that made her wish she'd wake up and discover she was only dreaming. But this, she realized as the initial stunned silence ended, was no dream.

"Who the hell are you?" she heard Stan demand plaintively. "Who is he?" he asked no one in particular. "Does anyone know who this madman is?"

Kali's soft, half-swallowed "I do" was drowned out by the general murmur of the crowd and crew and Jesse's own thundering response.

"I'll tell you who I am," he declared in a tone Kali recognized from the incident in the club. "I'm a friend of Kali's...a good friend. Too good a friend to stand around here watching her pose in this flimsy thing in the freezing cold."

Stan looked incensed. "She's getting paid to pose regardless of the temperature, and that flimsy thing happens to be a Clinton Ives original."

"Fine—let him try strutting around in it on a day like today."

A uniformed policeman who'd been standing on the edge of the crowd walked over to Stan. "Do you need some help here?"

"I'm not sure," Stan replied, eyeing the annoyingly possessive way Jesse was settling the coat over Kali's shoulders. "But don't go away."

"What do you think you're doing?" Kali demanded through clenched teeth as he fussed with the belt on her coat.

"Saving you from catching pneumonia."

"I do this all the time, and I have never caught pneumonia."

"A cold, then. I can't stand women who sniffle."

"And I can't stand men who think they have the right to tell the rest of the world what to do."

"I don't think I have the right to tell the rest of the world what to do...only you."

She met his flashy charmer's smile with a glare. "Well, think again. You can't come charging into a restricted area and interrupt a shoot just because you think it's too cold for me to work."

"I just did," he pointed out infuriatingly.

"Well, now you can just leave."

"Not without you. You don't even have enough sense to get out of the cold. But then if you've been standing out here since sunrise, your brain is probably frozen."

"Not that it's any of your business, but we do take breaks." She jerked a thumb toward the trailer dressing room.

"Good, take one now. Maybe if your lips turn from blue to red, I'll let you come back in a couple of hours."

"A couple of hou— You're out of your mind."

"That's what your friend over there seems to think."
Jesse cocked his head toward where Stan stood gaping. "So
why don't you indulge the madman—take a break."

"I don't *need* a break."

"Maybe not—but I think I do." Both Kali and Jesse
swung around at the sound of Stan's weary, slightly con
fused voice. "In fact, what I really need is a drink. Maybe
two. I think I'd already gotten all I needed before the interruption." He flicked a brief, disdainful glance at Jesse
before turning back to Kali with a weak smile. "Why don't
we call it a day? If I do come up short, we'll rebook for next
week. That is, of course, if the weather meets with your
approval."

"Oh, it will," Kali responded quickly. "I mean...just call
if you need any more shots."

"Right, love." He turned to issue instructions to the
crew, who had started folding up camp the second he'd
suggested calling it a day. Abruptly Stan stopped. "And,
Kali...you should really teach your friend there some
manners."

"Right, Stan," she forced out through gritted teeth. "I'll
work on it."

Jesse kept his eyes on Kali, the slight lift of his black
brows as suggestive as his low drawl. "Mmm. I can hardly
wait."

Responding with a "Don't bother," in a tone even frost-
ier than the air, Kali flounced up the trailer steps and inside, slamming the door behind her just to make sure he
got the message. When she emerged a half hour later,
wearing jeans and a bulky sweater beneath her coat, the
crowd had disappeared and Jesse was sitting alone on one
of the low stone benches. He stood at the sight of Kali.

"I thought I told you not to bother waiting," she said as
he stepped directly into her path.

"You did, but I knew you didn't really mean it." His friendly smile faded in the face of her outraged expression, and he rushed on before she could deliver her scathing opinion of his manners, his intelligence and his right to breathe the same air as normal, sane people. "Besides, you need me. When I told your friends I was driving you home, they took off."

A quick glance to where the rented limousine had been confirmed what he'd said. "I can't understand why they didn't stick around just to chat with you," drawled Kali, her tone dripping sarcasm.

Jesse shrugged, that crooked grin coming out of nowhere to steal some of her ire. "Me, either. I especially wanted to ask that skinny guy where he got his hat. Do you think I'd look good in a beret?"

"Stunning. It would hide that total void between your ears."

He sighed and shoved his hands into the pockets of his jeans. "You're angry."

"Angry? Whatever would make you think I'm angry?"

"I guess I'm just an overly sensitive guy." His offhand attempt at humor only fanned the flames.

"Right—about as sensitive as a rock. I mean, you did interrupt the shoot, screw up a very important assignment and make a fool out of me in front of one of the top photographers in the country, but I'm not angry."

"Good, then I'll drive you home."

"I'd rather crawl."

He caught her arm as she moved to step around him. "Kali, wait. I'm sorry I stuck my nose in, but I really thought I was helping."

"I don't need your help or anybody else's to tell me how to do my job. I know when I need a break, and it was insulting to have you insinuate that I don't." Her eyes flashed like dark sapphires. "How would you like it if I jumped onto the ice in the middle of a game and insisted the referee give you a chance to catch your breath?"

A dull red stain crept up his neck to cheeks. "You're right. I should have minded my own business. But do you know how hard it was to stand there and watch you freezing in that gown?"

"Yes, probably as hard as it was for me to sit in the stands watching you dodge pucks without a helmet." Seeing his eyes widen in surprise, Kali realized the impulsive retort might have revealed more about her feelings than she wished to. "Not that a blow to your head could do much damage," she added.

Jesse chuckled as he fell into step beside her. "Probably not, but it's still nice to know you care. My car is parked over there."

She jerked her arm from his hold. "And the taxi stand is over here."

"You're not taking a taxi."

Kali noticed that the hint of steely determination was back in his voice, and she quickened her pace—until his short, savage oath brought her to a halt. Her first thought when she turned to see him bent over, clutching his knee, was that this was some sort of stupid trick. But one look at his face, suddenly chalky white around his eyes, which were squeezed shut in pain, convinced her his pain was real.

Three quick steps carried her back to his side. "My God, Jesse, are you all right?"

"Fine." The word was forced through his clenched teeth.

"It doesn't look as if you're fine."

"I don't give a damn how it—" He broke off and attempted a conciliatory smile. "It's nothing...just a little muscle pull. It happened this morning at practice."

"Should you be walking on it?"

"Sure," he grunted. "Best thing for it—keeps me from stiffening up."

Kali looked on doubtfully as he massaged the knee, only slightly relieved to note that color was slowly returning to his face. "Do you think you should sit down for a minute?"

"Yeah. I'll be fine once I get to the car." He arrowed a quick glance her way. "That is, *if* I make it to the car. Would you mind giving me a hand?"

Kali hesitated. Despite the defiantly mischievous glint in his jade eyes, there was no doubt his pain was genuine, and people *were* beginning to stare at them strangely. It hardly seemed the time to insist on taking a taxi just to prove he couldn't order her around.

"All right," she said, "but I'll do the driving."

His brows slanted ominously. "Over my dead body."

"What a tempting thought," countered Kali sweetly, at the same time offering him the support of her arm. "I'm sure it could be arranged."

Jesse took it, straightening carefully. "I'd just as soon have it arranged as have a woman drive the Jag."

"Why you...caveman," she blurted in exasperation as he steered her toward the passenger side of the black Jaguar. The man even managed to limp in a determined, aggressive manner. Then she said smugly, "Just how do you propose to work the clutch if you can barely stand on that left leg?"

"Carefully," Jesse replied, swinging the door open for her with a smile that was still a little wilted around the edges. "Very, very carefully."

At least, she decided, when he was being careful his driving was easier on her nerves; she had only to squeeze her eyes shut in fervent prayer once during the ride to her place. Instead of parking in the garage, Jesse pulled up in front of the canopied brick building and started opening his door to come around and help her out.

Trying to ignore the quick stab of disappointment that his offer to drive her home had meant no more than that, Kali quickly reached out to catch his arm. "Jesse, please don't get out. I know what you said about not letting it stiffen up, but I still don't think you should be walking on that leg."

His mustache tilted above an endearingly sheepish grin. "You're probably right. That's why I didn't ask you to have lunch with me. I figure if I go home and rest it for a few hours, it'll stop throbbing and I'll feel good enough by tonight to take you to dinner. Somehow the thought of you and candlelight and a long night alone together appeals to me a whole lot more than a quick sandwich somewhere."

It appealed to Kali a whole lot more, too. Enough to make her forget her vow to be cautious. She was on the verge of agreeing when she remembered this was Monday.

"I'm sorry, Jesse," she said, amazed at how very true that was. "I've already made plans for tonight."

"With another man?"

She bit back a smile at the quick darkening of his expression and cupped her ear with one hand. "Do I hear the sound of someone pounding his chest?"

"I don't know. It depends on whether or not what I'm hearing is the sound of a woman trying to dodge the question."

"I'm not dodging...and I'm not seeing another man tonight. Not," she felt compelled to add haughtily, "that you have any right to ask."

"Haven't you noticed? I enjoy doing things I have no right to do. It adds spice to life." He grinned and reached over to slide his thumb along her nose. His skin felt warm and callused, and excitement that was totally out of proportion to the light touch started pulsing inside Kali. "I have no right to ask you to change your plans for me, either, but—"

Kali's firmly shaking head brought him up short. "I'm sorry, Jesse, but this is something I can't cancel out of."

He shrugged. "Then maybe I could sort of tag along."

The hopeful light in his eyes made it hard for her to tell him that was out of the question. It had taken her months to win the trust of Sandy Rogers, the autistic child she'd become involved with through her volunteer work. She couldn't jeopardize the progress they'd made by dragging Jesse along to their weekly get-together without preparing Sandy first...no matter how much she longed to be with him. "You can't come with me, Jesse. Not tonight." She hesitated, wondering if it would help if she explained who she was spending the evening with and why. But then she had no reason to think Jesse would be more understanding or accept her refusal any more graciously if he knew he was being passed over for an eight-year-old. "I am free if you'd like to have dinner tomorrow evening, though."

As soon as the words were out of her mouth she felt her cheeks heating up. My God! She had just asked Jesse McPherson for a date. Seriously this time, and she wasn't sure he would like that any better now than when she'd flashed the request from above the Colosseum scoreboard. He was scowling.

"Look," she began awkwardly, "forget I asked. If you're going to be busy—"

"It's not that I'm going to be busy," he broke in, sweeping a thick wave of dark hair from his forehead in a gesture that was rough and impatient. "The fact is I'm not even going to be here. The team is leaving tomorrow afternoon for a three-game road trip to Kansas City." He eyed her calculatingly. "If I asked you to come. . ."

Impulsively Kali leaned closer to silence him by pressing her fingertips against his lips. "I'd have to say no. So please don't ask." A smile tugged at the corners of her mouth. "You're doing much better, though. I would have expected that caveman inside to just grab my hair and drag me off with him."

"He's considering it. . .believe me." His breath warmed her fingers as he spoke, and when he finished speaking, he slid his tongue along the sensitive tips in a lingeringly, erotically moist caress.

Kali wasn't aware she'd closed her eyes until she opened them to find Jesse watching her. The undisguised longing in his gaze and the heat of his mouth against her fingertips unleashed desire she wasn't sure she should be feeling at all, never mind while sitting in a car on a very busy street in the middle of the day. She started to pull her hand away, but Jesse quickly covered it with his own and proceeded to treat her to the magic of his tongue once more. . .this time more slowly, each finger receiving lavish attention until she burned to feel that special, branding touch all over her body. The combination of his gently stroking tongue and the intent, hungry way he continued to look at her turned Kali's bones to marshmallow, and her thoughts to images that made her blush. It was definitely time to get out of the car.

"When will you be coming back?" she asked, her voice revealingly husky.

As an attempt to distract Jesse the question was a failure. He slowly drew her baby finger into the furnace of his mouth, then released it and strung nibbling kisses along her palm to the back of her wrist before replying. "Early next week."

"How early?"

He lifted his head to smile at her, and Kali knew he'd caught the breathless note in her question. "Monday."

"That's not nearly early enough," she softly admitted to him.

The excitement that gleamed in his eyes was very sensuous and *very* unsettling. "Maybe I'll get lucky and my leg will turn out to be broken. Then I won't have to go at all."

"Heaven forbid." Kali chuckled, rolling her eyes. "You'd be miserable company if you had to sit still and watch the game on television—you'd probably end up taking your frustrations out on me."

"Never." His growl told Kali he hadn't taken the quip as it had been intended. "Don't even joke about that. I know you think I'm rough—hell, it's no secret, but I would never hurt you. You do know that, don't you, Kali?"

Kali saw in his eyes the need to have her believe him wholeheartedly, and she wished she could. She had only been joking about his hitting her, but she wasn't sure Jesse wasn't capable of hurting people in other, deeper ways without even knowing he was doing it. She knew that if she loved him it would hurt her to watch him taking foolish chances and living up to the ruthless image that had been forged on the sports pages. Of course she wasn't in love with him, she reminded herself, so what he was really made no difference.

Reaching for her canvas tote bag, she met his narrowed gaze with a bright smile. "Of course you wouldn't hurt me...you're much too busy hurting yourself. I want you to promise me you'll take care of that leg."

A smile worked its way slowly across Jesse's face. "All right, Princess. He smiled slowly. "I'll let you sidestep my question this time, but someday you're going to look at me

in that same sexy way you did a few minutes ago and tell
me that you trust me...along with a whole lot of other
things I want to hear. I just hope you don't take too long
doing it. I hate waiting...especially for something I want
so badly."

"Patience," Kali informed him, calling on primness to
conceal the strange pleasure she derived from his words,
"is a virtue."

"Which is exactly why I've never bothered to cultivate
it." Circling the back of her neck with one hand, Jesse drew
her close to his chest. "I'll call you as soon as I get back on
Monday."

He finished the words against her mouth, kissing her
with an overwhelming possessiveness that merged his
breath and taste with hers and left Kali reeling. It wasn't
until he'd gone and she was on her way upstairs in the elevator that she remembered the swimsuit feature for
Sportsworld magazine. A week on location in Jamaica had
sounded glorious when she'd agreed to take the assignment. Now it sounded like grounds for a volcanic explosion. Pounding her tote bag against the metal wall, to the
combined confusion and amusement of her fellow riders,
she muttered a frustrated "Damn. I won't even be here on
Monday."

6

KALI TRIED UNSUCCESSFULLY to reach Jesse several times before leaving for her visit with Sandy. Afterward she spent an uncomfortable taxi ride to Sandy's house trying to decide which was more painful: imagining Jesse's reaction when he called after his road trip and discovered she wasn't around, or having to break the news to Sandy that she wouldn't be able to see her next Monday night.

A short while later, watching the pretty, brown-eyed girl mull over her assurances that nothing but an important modeling assignment could keep her away on their special day, Kali decided she'd rather deal with Sandy any day. Something told her the eight-year-old had accepted the disappointment a lot more maturely than old Mount McPherson was going to.

Kali had brought along a sticker book guaranteed to pique Sandy's newfound interest in horses. Once she had greeted the other Rogers children, who ranged in age from four months to ten years, the two of them sat at the family's big kitchen table, carefully arranging the stickers on the book's glossy pages. Kali chatted as they worked, following Sandy's doctor's advice—always giving her an opportunity to respond, but never pressing or demanding. As usual Sandy was cooperative and interested, but absolutely silent, and as they gave each other a giant hug before Sandy trotted upstairs to bed, Kali wondered if she was really helping the child at all.

She knew from talking with Sandy's parents and doctor that the girl had come a long way since she'd first been diagnosed as autistic. She no longer retreated into an impenetrable trance for seemingly no reason, or spent long periods absorbed in some simple, repetitive action like swaying or pounding on the floor. But she still didn't communicate verbally, and that hindered all other aspects of her life. She couldn't function in a normal classroom or make friends with the other children in the neighborhood, and Kali knew her behavior was a strain not only on her three brothers and sisters, but on her parents as well.

For Jenny Rogers's sake, Kali always attempted to end the evening by shedding the most positive light possible on her daughter's progress. Tonight was no exception, and as she and Jenny shared a cup of tea after the rest of the family had gone to bed, Kali flipped open the sticker book for Sandy's mother to see.

"Her attention span has improved remarkably, Jenny," she assured the plump brunette, whom worry had aged beyond her thirty-eight years. "When I first started working with her a year ago, she wouldn't even finish coloring one picture or sit through half a movie. Now she'll do a book like this cover to cover in one sitting, and last week she was as good as gold when I took her to that ice show."

Jenny nodded, hope mingling with concern in her eyes. "But still without saying a word. Sometimes I wonder if she ever will."

"She will," Kali insisted. "Maybe not next week, or even next month, but it will happen. I can see her confidence growing all the time, and you know that's half the battle. And she's becoming so inquisitive. Someday all the time and effort you've spent will click, and Sandy will do as much yakking as any other girl her age."

"I only hope you're right." Jenny's eyes closed briefly as she released a deep sigh, then she looked over at Kali with a rueful smile. "I don't know who's going to miss your visit more next week—Sandy or me. You're good for all of us, Kali. And I don't mean just the work you do with Sandy or the presents you're always bringing the kids, though God knows how many times I've told you not to."

"And I've told you," teased Kali, "that you're Sandy's mother, not mine...so don't go giving me orders."

Jenny laughed. "I swear you get fresher every week. But I still don't know what we'd do without you."

Kali responded with a self-conscious shrug and sipped her tea. Lately Jenny's warm expressions of gratitude had been making her more and more uncomfortable, and for good reason. Kali still hadn't mentioned a word about possibly retiring from modeling and returning home to North Dakota. The director of the volunteer program had assured Kali that, given enough notice, she could assign another volunteer to work with Sandy with as little threat to her progress as possible. Yet Kali knew she'd become more than a volunteer to Sandy and Jenny and the rest of the Rogers family. She was a friend.

Jenny had told her more than once that she looked forward all week to talking with someone who didn't spill milk all over the table or have to be burped afterward. Still, Kali was becoming more and more dissatisfied with her professional life each day. Sooner or later she would have to tell them about her plans. But not tonight, Kali decided, glancing at the worry lines creasing Jenny's pretty face.

She carried her empty cup to the sink and rinsed it out. "I guess I should get out of here and let you go to bed. You have to be up even earlier than I do in the morning."

"I suppose," Jenny said with a sigh. "By six-thirty I have to have lunches packed, beds made and breakfast for six on the table."

Kali groaned. "At that time I'm usually still trying to pry my eyes open enough to put my make-up on straight."

"Want to trade places?" the other woman asked wistfully.

"Believe me, after a day like today I'm tempted."

"Anytime. I think that's another reason I enjoy your visits so much—they're as close as I'm likely to get to all that glamour. I love hearing about the latest fashions and the trips...and the men." Her expression shifted from dreamy to frankly curious. "Are you still dating that soap-opera producer?"

Kali shook her head. "Not for weeks now—didn't I tell you the story of our last date?"

"No." Anticipation sparked in her eyes. "But I'm sure it's well worth waiting for."

"Well, you remember how romantic I told you he was? Always bringing me flowers and suggesting hansom-cab rides through the park in the moonlight?"

"Ah, yes...so he could admire the glow of your hair."

"Yeah, right." A cynical smile started at the corners of Kali's lips. "Well, during the last of his famous rides, he went from admiring the glow of my hair in the moonlight to tackling me in the back seat—much to the fascination of the kid who was trying to drive."

Jenny chuckled. "How very unromantic. What did you do?"

"Used a defensive move my brothers taught me back in high school." She patted her knee. "Tacky, but very effective."

Jenny quickly tempered her roar of laughter so as not to wake the children. "I can see why you decided not to see him again."

"Actually, he's the one who decided...he said I have no class. It's probably just as well," she added with a shrug, grinning broadly. "Once his toupee slipped I knew I would never feel the same about him."

"His toupee?" Jenny chortled. "Really?"

Kali nodded gleefully. "Yup—it did a nosedive when he bent over to clutch his—well, you get the picture."

"Vividly." Jenny wiped a tear from her eye, then advised unnecessarily, "Don't let it get you down. Mr. Right has to be out there somewhere."

"As a matter of fact, I did meet another sort of...interesting man a little while ago," Kali admitted impulsively, then sighed. "But I think he may actually be more of a Mr. Wrong."

Jenny took one look at the confusion and excitement on Kali's face and crossed to the stove. "Sit down," she said over her shoulder, "and I'll put the kettle back on."

During the next half hour, Kali revealed more to Jenny about Jesse and her feelings for him than she'd been aware of herself until then. A variety of conflicting emotions came through as she described their stormy first meeting and the rollercoasterlike path their relationship had taken since. Jenny alternately laughed and shook her head, and with her gentle, pointed questions forced Kali to examine angles and dimensions of her feelings that she would have preferred to leave safely in the shadows. Kali ended by relating how he'd demolished the photo session that afternoon.

"Of course *he* insisted he was rescuing me from freezing to death," she finished, aware of the reluctant amusement that penetrated her grumbling. "The man is unbelievably arrogant."

"But gallant."

"And ridiculously macho—I told you about that scene in the club."

"And charming and sexy and fun to be with. You also told me about the day you two spent together."

Kali smiled, then frowned. "One good day doesn't change the fact that he's basically very…volatile. If I wanted Mr. Excitement I would have stuck with that rock singer…you remember, the one with the earring and the braids? I'm looking for a man who's gentle and dependable and interested in sane, ordinary things, someone like Fred." At the mention of her husband, a small smile lit Jenny's face. "No one would ever confuse Fred with Mr. Excitement, that's for sure."

"Maybe not, but if you ask me, the fact that after twelve years and four kids you still smile that secret little smile just at the mention of his name is worth more than excitement…worth more than all the minks and jewels I've ever modeled."

"You don't think Jesse McPherson would give you reason for a secret little smile?"

"Not as often as he'd give me reason for cardiac arrest," Kali countered stubbornly.

"Maybe. But if he is as wrong for you as you claim, what is it about him that makes your eyes sparkle and your voice race—and jumbles your nerves enough that you shed half a box of napkins just talking about him?"

Kali followed her bemused glance to the pile of pale blue scraps on the table in front of her. She had to admit that was a good question, and when she put her coat on to leave a short while later, she was still searching for an answer that would sweep the affectionate, amused expression from her friend's face.

"How should I know what it is about the man that intrigues me?" she finally groaned in exasperation. "I only know he does. There, does that make you happy?"

"That's not what matters," Jenny replied, her quietly sympathetic tone reminding Kali a little of her own mother's. "What matters is that *you're* happy."

Kali had a lot of time during the week Jesse was away, and the week in Jamaica that followed, to contemplate Jenny's parting shot. While she basked on white sand beaches and lolled in gentle bubbling brooks—all for the benefit of the ever-present lens—she asked herself if she could be happy with a man like Jesse. The answer seemed to be an emphatic no.

The fast-paced life-style he thrived on was nothing but a burden to Kali, whereas she was certain he would consider her grand dreams for future happiness terminally boring. But just because she was coolly logical enough to tally up all the minuses didn't mean she had to like the final total...and her logic did absolutely nothing to quell a haunting sensation: whatever it was that was drawing her closer to Jesse, it was stronger than her will to resist.

Late Friday afternoon the photographer in charge of the shoot announced they were through, adding that *Sportsworld* magazine had invited the entire crew to stay on at the luxurious Silversword Manor for the rest of the weekend as their guests. The heavy-duty partying that was bound to ensue didn't tempt Kali at all, but ordinarily the prospect of two lazy days to do as she pleased on a tropical island would have.

Ordinarily.

Nothing about her desires and urges was ordinary these days. In fact, both had been downright wayward ever since Jesse had stormed into her life—or rather, honesty forced her to amend, since she'd stormed into his. Right now she wanted to see him much more than she wanted to wander through the open-air market in Ocho Rios, or rent a motorbike to explore the island's rugged coastline.

Telling herself all the way to New York that she was crazy to pass up two days' vacation to rush back to a man whose mood was probably as stormy as the weather forecast, Kali took a taxi to the small island airport and bought a ticket for the next flight to New York. Several hours later she stepped out of John F. Kennedy Airport into a swirl of gently falling snow, immensely thankful that the balmy temperatures she'd left behind hadn't lulled her into packing her heavy coat instead of carrying it.

First thing when Kali reached her apartment, she picked up the phone to retrieve her messages from the answering service. She listened politely to the operator reciting the list of calls that had come in before and after the only one that mattered...the one that told her Jesse had called last Monday just as he'd promised, and received her message that she would be gone a week, along with the name and telephone number of the hotel where she was staying.

It irked her slightly that he hadn't seen fit to call her there just to say hello. That bit of proof that Jesse wasn't the sort of man to bother with trivial courtesies reinforced an image of him that should be making her very uneasy. Kali didn't feel uneasy at all. She felt restless, a little anxious, full of a heady anticipation. The feeling mushroomed as she went about unpacking and reviving herself with a long, hot bath...all the while conducting a one-woman debate on the merits of calling Jesse just to casually announce she'd returned home a couple of days early.

Finally dredging up the courage to act on the impulse, she let his phone ring a good twenty times before acknowledging the obvious. She dropped the receiver back into the cradle with a frustrated slam. As a result of her newly developed devotion to reading every word about pro hockey in the sports section, she knew the Bandits weren't playing that night, and they weren't on the road. What she *should* have known, she told herself irritably, was that Jesse wasn't the type to sit home cooling his heels on a Friday night just because she was out of town.

She was dragging a wide-toothed comb through her wet hair—trying to work off the unbidden jealousy that accompanied fantasies of how he was spending the evening—when the buzzer sounded. Flinging the comb onto the coffee table, Kali nearly ran across the room to the intercom speaker, perversely knowing, even before she heard the doorman's detached announcement, that Jesse was there to see her.

"Of course send him up," she instructed, aiming for a nonchalant tone that wouldn't betray the fact that her heart was suddenly spinning like a top.

"Right away, Miss Spencer."

Right away. Kali glanced down at the old red plaid flannel robe she'd pulled on after her shower, and after quickly gauging how long she usually had to wait for one of the building's two elevators to reach her floor, decided she had time to change before Jesse banged on her door. Throwing open the double doors of her closet, she stared at the twin rows of hangers that held worn-out jeans and slinky evening gowns and everything in between. The first thing her hand landed on was hurriedly dragged out and tossed on the quilt-covered queen-size bed; then she paused with her robe unbelted and halfway off one arm.

"What are you thinking of?" she muttered, eyeing the well-worn jeans and navy turtleneck sweater. They were comfortable, but hardly what she wanted to be wearing when Jesse saw her for the first time in almost two weeks.

She jerked the robe up and turned back to the closet, searching for something a little bit more   alluring. A pair of dark green velveteen slacks and a white lace blouse quickly joined the jeans on the bed. The instant they hit the quilt Kali frowned. *Too* alluring. After all, her hair was still wet, indisputable evidence that she hadn't been planning an elegant evening on the town.

A pair of taupe wool slacks were added to the growing pile before she remembered they itched, and in desperation grabbed the tailored gray corduroys that were halfway between comfortable and dressy. She was still searching frantically for the striped cotton sweater to match when a knock landed on the front door. It sounded like Jesse—firm, impatient—and Kali froze. A second knock, sounding even more like Jesse, freed her from her spell, and she lunged for the gray slacks, only to jam the zipper halfway up in her haste.

Quickly she stepped out of them. She was eyeing the jeans on the bed in a new, somewhat fevered light when he knocked again, answering her silent question; she didn't dare keep him waiting a little longer while she slipped them on. Belting the robe tightly, she did the best she could to fluff her wet hair, then went to let him in.

Despite her racing pulse, she wasn't at all prepared for the way her mouth went dry and her stomach flipped just at the sight of him. It took a few seconds to manage even a ridiculously winded-sounding "Hi."

Jesse propped one shoulder carelessly against the doorjamb and ran his eyes in a slow, burning perusal from her wet head to the tips of her bare toes. "All the way over here from the airport I wondered if I should have called first to tell you I was coming. Now I'm glad I didn't."

His soft, rough-edged voice and his gaze of sheer male approval both sent an unfamiliar shock wave rippling through Kali, and she was torn between tugging the robe higher to cover her throat or lower to hide her toes. Fighting both childish reactions, she smiled and opened the door a little wider.

"Come on in—it will only take me a second to change."

Jesse followed her in and closed the door, then grabbed her hand as she turned toward her bedroom. "Don't change. I like what you're wearing a whole lot better than any Clinton Ives original."

"Because it's so nice and warm?" she teased.

He reached out to stroke the curve of her hip. "I admit it's making me feel nice and warm, but I think what I like best about it is that it makes you seem so...accessible."

The desire in his voice made Kali think changing was more a matter of self-defense than good manners, but Jesse was already pulling her toward the sofa. Fighting the clamorings of her sensible nature, she trailed willingly.

It was hard to think sensibly when every nerve in her body was short-circuiting. She was tinglingly aware of the tough warmth of the hand holding hers, the faint cedar scent of his after-shave, and the way the melting snowflakes glittered like diamonds in his raven hair. He looked taller and broader and even more appealing than she'd remembered. Clad in snug black denims and a gray, kid-leather jacket that rode his lean hips, he posed a very real, very virile challenge. Somehow she'd hazed over that impression of him in her daydreams. Even now Kali swallowed hard and tried to ignore it.

"Did you plan on staying?" she asked, her voice tinctured with amusement as he lowered himself to the sofa.

When his eyes darkened as if she was issuing an invitation, she prodded, "Your jacket, Jesse. Would you like to take it off?"

"Only if you promise not to bolt into the bedroom and change your clothes the second I let go of your hand."

"I promise...but only to keep you from dripping on the upholstery."

He watched her pat the pale gray-and rose striped velvet and sighed. "That's not quite the loving, trusting response I'd hoped for, but at this point I'll take whatever I can get."

"'At this point?'" echoed Kali as she deposited the jacket on the brass coatrack by the door. "Sounds as if you've had a rough day."

"More like a rough two weeks," he corrected in a dry tone that left Kali in no doubt about whom he held responsible for his misery.

She smoothed the robe over her curled-up legs. "That's a pity," she said with studied obliqueness. "You should try getting away for a few days. I can vouch for the fact that Jamaica is beautiful at this time of the year."

"So can I."

The feeling in his tone caused Kali's eyes to widen, and she belatedly wondered why he'd come here straight from the airport if the team wasn't on the road. "You don't mean..."

"That I went all the way to Jamaica looking for you?" he finished when her voice dried up. "I sure did. When I got back here on Monday and found out you were gone, my first impulse was to fly down there and drag you back...but I fought it."

"That shows admirable self-control."

His derisive chuckle seemed self-directed. "Not really...I just couldn't stand the thought of all the stupid caveman digs you'd make. So I decided to take your advice and try being patient. And you know what? I learned something."

Kali eyed him warily, not certain she wanted to ask exactly what he'd learned, not when the knowledge inspired that almost feral gleam in his dark green eyes.

"I learned," he continued, edging closer to her on the sofa, "that I was right all along...I hate being patient...and I hate making sacrifices, and if I can help it I don't plan on doing either ever again. Particularly where you're concerned."

"Is that what you followed me to Jamaica to tell me?"

"I didn't risk being fined by skipping practice to fly all the way down there to *tell* you anything. Although a few choice things did come to mind when I arrived at that hotel and was informed you'd checked out a few hours earlier."

"I can imagine."

"I'm sure you can't," he said dryly. "And the situation only got worse when I stopped in the hotel bar to kill time before catching the next flight back here. A few of your co-workers were there partying, and the bartender couldn't take his eyes off them...except for the time it took to tell me that I'd just missed the foxiest looking one of all. He told me in great detail about this tall, blond model and how he'd spent his afternoons off, all week, watching her work."

His voice was too soft, his drawl too casual, and Kali found herself forcing an uneasy smile. "We did attract some pretty big crowds of onlookers."

"I'll bet. He especially liked the day you wore the black bathing suit...you know, the one-piece job with no back and almost no front."

Kali knew, all right. That was the suit that had led her to the sour conclusion that the nation's number-one sports magazine was more interested in high-priced cheesecake than high fashion. She'd posed in it, anyway, out of a deep-rooted sense of professional responsibility, but made a mental note that if by some horrible twist of fate she was still earning a living this way when *Sportsworld* shot next year's bathing-suit feature, she would not be available.

Now, under Jesse's relentless stare, she could feel her cheeks heating more than they had that day on the beach. "I guess it was a little...scant in places."

His half smile was sardonic. "In all the right places, according to the bartender."

"You don't have to sound so snide. It's not a bathing suit I would choose for myself, but it was part of an assignment I'd agreed to do." She shrugged, annoyed at herself for sounding so defensive. "It's just a job."

"Some job. One week you get to freeze, and the next you have to lie around half-naked while a bunch of perverts ogle you."

"Real glamorous, huh?"

He scowled, not catching the rueful note in her voice. "I guess that's all that counts. Tell me, though, why didn't you stick around on the island with your friends and soak up some more glamour? It looked as if they had more than enough male admirers to go around."

You, she almost blurted out. *You're the reason I couldn't wait to get back here to the slushy streets and icy sidewalks.* She was stopped cold by the look in his eyes, the flaring of an emotion fierce and elemental. Then, with a flash of intuition just as elemental, Kali realized he wasn't angry; he was jealous. She wasn't sure it said a lot for her character, but the revelation sent shivers of pure delight coursing through her.

"Jesse," she began, straining not to sound pleased or amused, "are you by any chance jealous?"

"Jealous?" The question hit Jesse like a blow to the midsection, and his dark brows levered up in astonishment.

Neither in the bar nor on that damned endless plane ride back here had he bothered to tag a name onto the raw feeling that churned inside and seemed to wear every nerve in his body to the breaking point. He just knew that the thought of other men seeing more of Kali than he'd even so much as glimpsed filled him with a burning, impotent fury that made it hard to breath.

Thoughts of Kali filled him with another feeling, as well. Beyond desire, which he was very familiar with, beyond need. Which he wasn't. He hadn't searched for a name for this other feeling, yet now he wondered if subconsciously he'd been afraid of finding the only word that fitted. Could he really be in love with Kali? So soon? Without ever having actually made love to her?

He looked at the teasing glints in her blue eyes, at her soft, expressive mouth, and the smile she was trying so hard to rein in. The idea was a lot more credible than he would have imagined. It was also very unnerving, and for now he'd settle for her definition of the whole mess of unfamiliar feelings.

"All right," he allowed finally, crossing his long legs at the ankle in an attempt to appear casual. "Maybe I am a little jealous."

"Looks like more than maybe to me."

"Maybe it's a little more than maybe."

"How much more than maybe?"

"Do you realize this is an absolutely absurd conversation?"

"I guess. Maybe we should talk about something else."

He grinned, a wicked flash of white teeth. "*Maybe* we shouldn't talk at all."

Kali's eyes widened, and a temptingly moist tongue slid over her bottom lip, fanning the fire burning deep inside Jesse.

"We could play Trivial Pursuit again," she offered. "Except I don't have it."

"Thank God for small favors." Weaving his fingers through her hair, he explored the soft angle of her jaw with his lips...lightly, as if she were a rare, timid bird not to be frightened away.

Kali trembled. "I do have Scrabble, though."

"I can't spell."

"Yahtzee?"

He lifted her hair to kiss underneath.

"I can't count, either."

"Chess?"

"Boring."

His teeth raked gently over her earlobe.

"Actually it's very st-stimulating."

"Actually, Princess, so are you...but you talk too much."

Very carefully he tipped her shoulders, the slight pressure sending her floating down onto the sofa cushion.

"Jesse, I don't think..."

"Good—I'd much rather you just lie back and feel."

"But this will only complicate things...there's still so much I don't know about you."

He swept his hand from her shoulder to her hip and back, marveling at the perfect arrangement of curves and valleys. "That's impossible...my life's an open book. I'm six foot two, one hundred ninety-five pounds. I love jazz and chocolate, hate push-ups and women who talk when I'm trying to make love to them. Anything else you need to know?"

GET 4 BOOKS
A CUDDLY TEDDY
AND A MYSTERY GIFT

Return this card, and we'll send you 4 Mills & Boon romances, absolutely FREE! We'll even pay the postage and packing for you!

We're making you this offer to introduce to you the benefits of Mills & Boon Reader Service: FREE home delivery of brand-new Mills & Boon romances, at least a month before they're available in the shops, FREE gifts and a monthly Newsletter packed with special offers and information.

Accepting these FREE books places you under no obligation to buy, you may cancel at any time, even after receiving just your free shipment.

Yes, please send me 4 free Mills & Boon romances, a cuddly teddy and a mystery gift as explained above. Please also reserve a Reader Service subscription for me. If I decide to subscribe, I shall receive 6 superb new titles every month for just £11.40 postage and packing free. If I decide not to subscribe I shall write to you within 10 days. The free books and gifts will be mine to keep in any case. I understand that I am under no obligation whatsoever. I may cancel or suspend my subscription at any time simply by writing to you.

Ms/Mrs/Miss/Mr ⎯⎯⎯⎯⎯⎯⎯⎯⎯⎯⎯ 10A4R

Address ⎯⎯⎯⎯⎯⎯⎯⎯⎯⎯⎯⎯⎯⎯⎯

⎯⎯⎯⎯⎯⎯⎯⎯⎯⎯⎯⎯⎯⎯⎯⎯⎯⎯⎯⎯

⎯⎯⎯⎯⎯⎯⎯⎯⎯⎯ Postcode⎯⎯⎯⎯⎯⎯

Signature⎯⎯⎯⎯⎯⎯⎯⎯⎯⎯⎯⎯⎯⎯
I am over 18 years of age.

Get 4 books
a cuddly teddy and
mystery gift FREE!

SEE BACK OF CARD FOR DETAILS

Mills & Boon Reader Service,
FREEPOST
P.O. Box 236
Croydon
CR9 9EL

No
stamp
needed

"Yes," she shot back, both hands pressed against his slowly descending shoulders, "how's your knee…and why don't you wear a helmet when you play?"

Jesse detected desire infiltrating her determination not to be affected by his seduction. He chuckled against the soft skin of her throat. "Why should I wear a helmet on my knee?"

"I mean on your head."

"My head is fine."

"That's debatable. Why don't you?"

"Debate?"

"Wear a helmet?"

"It messes my hair up."

"Be serious."

"Believe me, I'm trying," he groaned, and stopped nibbling on her neck to stare down at her with passion-glazed eyes. "The real reason I don't wear one is because it's hot and uncomfortable and hinders my technique—just as you're doing right now."

Before she could respond, Jesse brought his body fully on top of her, his patience spent, his need for her fierce.

He wanted to devour her, transform resistance into eagerness and drown himself deep in her sweetness. He settled for allowing his tongue to trace the delicate shape of her lips, before capturing them completely in a kiss that made him tremble with the hunger he was determined to keep in check. But damn, that was hard.

His body was reacting to Kali as if he were sixteen again, instead of an experienced thirty. And Jesse knew that being impatient was the surest way to scare Kali off…maybe permanently.

There was fire beneath her gentleness and reticence. Jesse wanted that fire for his own. But, lifting his mouth from hers to reexplore the line of her throat, he reminded himself that hers was not the sort of fire you could ever possess by storming the hearth. It would have to be sheltered and nurtured as carefully as one would a candle in the wind, because he cared about Kali and her own pleasure. In the end, her passion would burn far brighter and far longer than any quick flash and be worth the effort it was costing him now to reassure her with his strength.

Jesse felt Kali's arms curl around his neck, pulling him closer, and her breath warmed his ear as she moaned, a soft, yearning sound. This time when his mouth closed hungrily over hers, she responded by parting her lips and sliding her tongue teasingly against his.

It was Jesse's turn to moan.

Kali would have smiled at his passionate gruffness if her mouth hadn't been involved in Jesse's unique brand of ravishment. The way he was kissing her was as much a contradiction as the man himself. Briefly Kali wondered at the strangely harmonious blending of charm and arrogance, gentleness and aggression.

Then the moment for wondering was past, and she was swept to a realm where she could only feel. . .and respond. Jesse's hands had slipped lower, and his hips were moving against hers in slow, teasing circles. The new sensations that had been whipping through her with hurricane force seemed to coalesce suddenly in her pelvis, which cushioned his hardness. Instinctively Kali reached for the steady anchor of his broad shoulders as she arched, obeying some ancient call to intimacy that needed no reason and knew no restraint.

Lifting up a bit, Jesse watched her closely as he untied the belt at her waist with deliberation, then let the ends drift to the sofa beside her. Kali knew his leisurely approach was intended to give her a chance to stop him if that's what she wanted. At that moment it wasn't at all what she wanted.

She watched in silence as his hands moved to the edge of her robe. They were beautiful hands, strong, dusted with short, dark hairs, and they touched her with an almost reverent sensuality as he peeled the material off her shoulders, leaving her covered only by white lace panties and the heat of his gaze.

"Kali...you're beautiful, even more beautiful than I'd imagined." His voice was raspy with emotion, his eyes ablaze with silver-green fire.

"When you look at me I feel beautiful," she whispered shyly, her breath catching deep inside as he enclosed the fullness of her breasts in his hands. She could feel the tips hardening, responding to the teasing caress of his palms. "And when you touch me I— Oh, Jesse, I can't breathe."

"Then take my breath...take all of me." He kissed her with rough ardor, staggering her senses with the force of his loving. "Oh, sweet Kali, let me feel your fire...."

He breathed the words into her mouth as his tongue stabbed and tangled with hers. Shock waves of excitement jagged through Kali as his kiss grew deeper, more probing and his fingers trailed over her ribs and lower, stroking her through the sheer silk panties. Then he levered up to grab her hands and bring them to the top button of his white shirt.

"Unbutton my shirt." It was part plea, part command, spoken in a tone heavy with desire. "I want to feel your skin sliding against mine."

Kali worked her way down the row of buttons with fingers that trembled as much as the rest of her. It had been longer than a long time since a man had made her quiver like this, since she'd been this hungry for a man. It had been forever, and she hazily acknowledged the irony: Jesse had the power to unleash a reckless sensuality she hadn't even known she possessed.

She spread his shirt open and let her fingers dance over his skin. Jesse smiled at her in lazy amusement as she explored the shape and texture of him with loving fascination. His eyes narrowed slightly when she teased his nipples to erectness, and Kali could feel the pounding of his heart accelerate furiously when she leaned forward to touch them with her tongue. But it wasn't until she began tracing the pattern of curling dark hairs that flared then tapered as it neared his belt that he became frustrated with his inactive role.

He pinned her to the sofa with a kiss that claimed and demanded, making Kali feel as though she was poised at the edge of some dangerous unfamiliar cliff, even before he pulled away to look at her with an intensity that bordered on desperation.

"A few weeks ago you told me you weren't ready for this to happen," he gasped. "Are you ready now, Kali?"

The disjointed words penetrated the sensual spell he'd woven around her. Kali blinked, disoriented, as she struggled to make sense of this shift in his behavior.

"Ready. . ." she echoed softly. "I'm not sure —"

"That's what I thought," he snapped before she could finish. "Well, you'd better be sure. I need to know what you're thinking. I'm not made of steel, for God's sake. . ."

7

No, HE DEFINITELY wasn't made of steel, Kali reflected, resurfacing more with each second. Jesse was glaring steadily at her.

He was made of taut, warm flesh and unyielding muscle. And his lovemaking moves were so accomplished, persuasive...indescribably pleasurable. But did they go any further than technique with Jesse? Was he even capable of the tender, fragile emotions she was beginning to feel toward him? Kali didn't have enough firsthand experience of either love or lust to be one hundred percent certain. Long ago she had promised herself that certain was exactly what she would be before ever again giving herself completely to a man.

As she struggled to jam her arms back into the tangled sleeves of her robe, Jesse heaved a defeated sigh and levered into a sitting position to help her. She retied the belt and haphazardly smoothed her hair, all the while searching for something to say that would break the dark silence between them. It didn't help that her mind was vibrating with doubts and questions she should have dealt with sometime before this moment. During the two weeks she and Jesse had been apart, it had been easy to gloss over the differences in their personalities and life-styles. She had simply barred from her fantasies the disquieting side of him, the side that flared to life so magnificently on the ice…the Jesse who was rough and aggressive and who played to win, at all costs.

It would also be foolhardy to let her physical response to him blind her to the fact that their futures seemed to be charted on divergent courses. No doubt they could have a fabulous casual fling, and maybe he would be comfortable with that. Kali never could be. She had no intention of being just one more easy lay for Jesse McPherson. Because she had an unnerving suspicion that her hunger for him wouldn't be satisfied in one night, or a hundred, maybe not even in a lifetime.

She shifted to face him, debating whether to approach the situation with the truth or a joke. One look at his granite-hard face, his firm chin, told her a glib remark wouldn't be well received.

"Jesse, I'm sorry." She placed her hand lightly on his arm. "I shouldn't have let things get so out of hand."

Remarkably, amazingly, he smiled.

"It's very generous of you to try to shoulder the blame," he responded dryly. "But I did have a little something to do with what happened." His fingertips lifted to ride the crest of her cheek in an idle caress. "Kali, I meant it when I promised not to steamroller you into bed, but you may have to remind me of my good intentions from time to time."

Kali rubbed her cheek against him, marveling at the contentment she felt just being held in his strong arms, listening to the sure, steady beat of his heart.

"God, I want you, Kali," he whispered against her hair. "But I also want you to want me…I want you to be sure of your feelings."

She lifted her head, briefly tempted to tell him that her feelings weren't the problem, that only her common sense stood between them and the ecstasy he'd let her glimpse a few minutes earlier. She welcomed the distraction of the sight outside her fourteenth-story window. The snow that had been a light flurry an hour earlier was now a solid curtain of white.

"Jesse, look," she blurted awkwardly, "it's snowing."

Jesse turned to gaze out the window, breaking into a grin that mirrored the excitement that always spiraled inside her at the first snow of the season.

"It looks as if that big storm they forecast for next week decided to come a little early," he remarked cheerfully. "I guess it'll be a white Christmas, after all."

Instantly Kali's thousand-watt smile dimmed. "Oh, no. I forgot all about Christmas."

"Don't worry," Jesse said with a chuckle. "It's not until next Wednesday—you still have plenty of time for last-minute shopping."

"I didn't forget about shopping. I've been shopping and mailing packages home for weeks now...but if it snows this hard next week, *I* won't be able to get there."

"Sure you will. They'll put extra crews on to keep the airports open for the holidays. You'll get home."

"But will I get back?" she moaned, sinking back on the sofa, her arms folded dejectedly. "In time for the booking I have scheduled for first thing the Friday after Christmas."

"What is it this time? Bikinis in the snow?"

Kali was too preoccupied to notice the sardonic lift of his brows.

"No—furs at Saratoga Springs. Oh, what difference does it make, anyway?" she grumbled. "It's still going to ruin my plan to go home for Christmas. Even if the New York airport is open, if there's a storm predicted for the Midwest, I won't be able to chance not getting back here in time." Kali knew she was pouting childishly, but that didn't make it any easier to stop. "This will be the first time I've ever spent Christmas away from home."

"Then why the hell did you agree to the job in the first place?'

Kali shrugged. "The agency put pressure on me. Besides, it's my last booking for Bently's Mints, and I suppose I just wanted to get it out of the way."

So there wouldn't be any loose threads in case her plan to retire took shape sooner than she anticipated, she refrained from adding. She hadn't told anyone about that yet—and wouldn't until she'd decided exactly when she would be leaving. Despite her growing desire to resume what she couldn't help thinking of as her "real life," she was finding it difficult to pick an arbitrary date to walk away from the five years she'd spent in New York.

Sometimes she thought enrolling for next fall's semester at the University of North Dakota had a nice, sensible ring to it. But on bad days, getting there in time for the summer session sounded even better. With a start she realized that her burgeoning feelings for Jesse might change all that.

Distracted, she forced a smile as he reached over to rub the back of her neck.

"There's no sense worrying about it now," he advised soothingly. "You know that old saying about the weather...if you don't like it—"

"Just wait a minute," she finished along with him. "I happen to know every old saying. Just as I *know* I'm going to be snowed in here for Christmas."

Hard on the heels of that miserable thought came an enticement. Spending Christmas snowed in with Jesse might offer some very worthwhile compensations. Kali wouldn't have thought anything could brighten the prospect of her first Christmas away from her family, but she was almost smiling as she asked lightly, "What are you planning to do for the holidays, Jesse?"

She might have imagined the sudden tightening of his expression, but Kali didn't think so.

"I'll be going home," he answered shortly.

She nodded, then added casually, "Unless of course, you get snowed in, too."

She was certain she wasn't imagining the tight, hard line his mouth had become. "Snow or no snow I have to go home. And speaking of home—" Kali's heart plummeted as he stood "—I guess I should be heading there now, before I get snowed in here for the night."

"You could sleep on the sofa," she offered as he drew her to her feet beside him.

Jesse shook his head. "No, I couldn't. I could never sleep knowing you were right in the next room." His eyes dropped with interest to her robe. "What do you sleep in, anyway?"

"A bed."

His interest surged. "That's all?"

"That's none of your business."

"Yet."

"Yet," Kali relented softly, loving the thoroughly wicked smile the word brought to his lips.

Jesse lowered his head, his mouth moving over hers in a kiss that was blatantly possessive and left them both straining for breath. Holding her face between his hands, he stroked her swollen bottom lip with the side of his thumb. "Soon, Kali. Very, very soon."

It wasn't a question or a threat, simply a statement of fact. Kali nodded slowly, then walked with him to retrieve his jacket from the hall tree.

He paused in the middle of zipping it. "I almost forgot—I wanted to ask you if you'd like to come with me to see *The Nutcracker* on Monday night."

"You mean the ballet?"

His dark mustache twisted sardonically at her amazed tone.

"No, the midget wrestling version—of course I mean the ballet. And if you make even one stupid joke about cavemen in tutus I'll rescind the invitation."

"In that case I'll just say yes, I'd love to go." She put a hand up to stop his lips when they were about an inch from hers. "But did you say Monday night?"

"Right...don't tell me you've already made plans?"

Kali nodded. "With. . .a friend. Could I bring her along?" she asked hopefully, then bit her lip. "Unless, of course, you've already bought the tickets."

"As long as your friend is a *her*, I suppose I can buy another ticket."

Kali chuckled. "She's not only a her, she's also only eight years old." Taking a deep breath, she added, "Jesse, I think I should warn you that Sandy is also autistic. That means—"

"I know what it means," he interjected easily. "And no warning is necessary. If she's a friend of yours, I'll be glad to have her come with us."

Eyes blazing with a new warmth, Kali smiled up at him. "Thank you. I know Sandy will be thrilled when I tell her." Her excitement dimmed as she bit her bottom lip worriedly. "Won't it be hard to get three seats together this close to the performance?"

"Excruciatingly. In fact, I'll probably have to trade the Jag to some sleazy scalper for them."

"I'm sorry, Jesse. Just forget I mentioned it."

"I can't forget it...I can't forget anything you've ever said to me. And I'll get the three seats together." He smoothed the hair back from her face, his voice changing to the drawl that sent shivers racing along her spine. "Kali, don't you know I'd sell my soul to make you happy?"

Feeling as though Roman candles were shooting off inside, Kali patted his chest easingly. "That's nice, Jesse, but I don't think a scalper's going to be much interested in your soul."

"Then I'll just have to come up with something else. Don't worry—" he kissed her quickly before moving out into the hallway "—I'll get Sandy a ticket...I'm rich, and I'm desperate."

THE BANDITS' SCHEDULE for the next two days was crammed with practice sessions, in preparation for Sunday night's game with their leading rival. Jesse's pivotal role in their last-minute victory that night left him in high spirits, but exhausted. Kali began to rethink the wisdom of his theory about the trials and tribulations of juggling two high-pressure careers. It was beginning to seem that whenever she was up, he was down...when he was here, she was gone.

She probably wouldn't have been feeling so bad if she hadn't still been stewing over Friday night. Absence might well make the heart grow fonder, she decided after a weekend of only scattered moments together and unfinished conversations, but uncertainty took all the fun out of being with Jesse. And uncertain was how she felt after Friday night.

Jesse's blunt announcement that he was going home for Christmas, come hell or high water, didn't say a lot for his desire to be with her. Of course she couldn't blame him for wanting to spend time with his family. Nor could she expect him to change plans that had probably been made as long ago as her own. But he could have had the decency to look a little regretful, or added that he would miss her.

Kali was certain she was going to miss him. His presence added colors to her life that she hadn't even known were missing. He made her feel beautiful in a way other men never had and all the top cover assignments in the world never could. And he made her feel desirable...not as if she was merely a prize to be displayed. He made her *feel* desire, too, great white-hot explosions of it whenever he touched her. They never disappeared entirely, but were only banked to a low burn that flared again at the slightest thought of him. For Kali, her reactions were the biggest eye-opener of all.

She arranged for Sandy to come to her apartment early Monday evening so that they could have some time alone together before Jesse arrived. While they were waiting, Kali told her the story of *The Nutcracker* and a little about Jesse so she would be prepared for both. To Kali's cautiously expressed hope that the three of them could share more good times together in the future, Sandy responded with a small smile. Primed by Jenny, no doubt, thought Kali, but it was still rewarding to see her opening herself up to new experiences instead of shying away from them.

After sharing a homemade pizza for supper, Kali helped Sandy don the lacy pink dress she'd brought to wear to the ballet, then left her watching a Black Beauty rerun while she showered and dressed. The lines of the velvet dress she'd chosen were simple: a demure scalloped neckline, full sleeves softly gathered just below the elbow and a wide satin sash at the waist. The effect, Kali decided, viewing the result in her dresser mirror, was exactly the one she wanted, sensually alluring without being overpowering.

The rich emerald color highlighted her creamy skin, and the delicate gathers emphasized the curve of breasts and hips that several snippy photographers had criticized as a little *too* full for a high-fashion model. Kali smiled. She didn't care if every photographer in New York, as well as the whole fashion-magazine-reading public, thought that. She had more than a hunch that Jesse McPherson wouldn't agree, and with each passing day Jesse, what he thought and said and did, was becoming more and more important in her world.

When the doorman buzzed to announce that their escort was downstairs waiting, Kali quickly grabbed both their coats and hustled Sandy off to the elevator. The little girl clung to her hand all the way down to the lobby, and as the doors slid open Kali knew an instant of piercing anxiety, worrying if she was doing the right thing, after all, by bringing Sandy along. Maybe, subconsciously, she was testing Jesse...trying to see if he would react to Sandy with the dazzling charm she knew he was capable of, or with the selfish arrogance of a man not used to making sacrifices of any kind. It was, she realized belatedly, a risky gamble...for all of them.

The moment they stepped from the elevator, Jesse straightened from his lounging position by the door and started across the busy lobby toward them. As he moved with the strong, graceful stride that was his alone, his gaze was riveted on Kali, sweeping over her in a frankly sensual perusal that left her breathless.

"You're beautiful," he said softly when he finally reached her side.

Kali smiled. "So are you."

It was true. The dark charcoal suit, white silk shirt and subtly patterned crimson silk tie added a dash of elegance that was devastating when combined with his virile good looks. Kali caressed the angles of his face and the freshly tamed waves of his dark hair with a loving gaze.

"In fact," she added with teasing decisiveness, "you're easily the most gorgeous man I've ever seen."

Jesse reacted to the compliment with an unexpectedly flustered smile and let his gaze drift down to Sandy, who was standing patiently by Kali's side.

"Jesse, this is my friend Sandy," Kali began, feeling a crushing wave of relief and adoration for him as he dropped to a crouch and smiled brightly at the little girl watching him with wary brown eyes.

"Hi there, Sandy. I guess I'm just about the luckiest guy in the whole city tonight, because it looks as if I get to escort *two* beautiful ladies to the ballet." He held out his hand, and after a brief hesitation Sandy amazed Kali by slipping hers into it for a quick shake. "Do you like the ballet, Sandy?"

Kali held her breath as the little girl contemplated him in silence.

"Okay," Jesse continued after a few seconds. His tone was blessedly neutral, without a trace of impatience or— even worse—pity. "I guess for now you're going to let me do most of the talking, but someday I want to hear all about how you and Kali spend Monday nights. Is it a deal?"

Sandy's eyes didn't hold the shuttered, aloof expression strangers usually merited, yet she still didn't say a word. Kali issued a silent prayer that Jesse wouldn't make the mistake many people did, by pressing her or trying to cajole her into answering. He didn't.

"Remember, I'm counting on you, Sandy." With that he straightened and reached for the coats Kali was clutching. He helped Sandy with hers first, then settled the satin-lined black velvet cape over Kali's shoulders with a squeeze that was light but eloquent. He didn't mind. In fact, he seemed to be genuinely pleased to have Sandy along. That simple fact seemed to topple the last stone in Kali's sturdy wall of resistance. Her heart sang so loudly she barely heard him asking if she'd mind taking a taxi to the theater.

"It'll be more comfortable," he explained, "and we won't have to worry about parking."

Kali nodded, more than willing to agree with anything he suggested in her current, floating-on-air mood.

Jesse proved to be a competent if somewhat offbeat tour guide as the taxi crept through city traffic made even crazier than usual by holiday shoppers. He pointed out places and people along the way with comical asides and zestfully related personal anecdotes that even had Sandy giggling by the time they reached the City Center on west Fifty-fifth Street.

Kali flashed him an appreciative smile as they were ushered to three seats in the second row.

"Do you still have the Jaguar?" she asked. "Or is some sleazy scalper now riding around the city in style?"

"I still have the Jag." When she feigned a sigh of relief, he added, "Of course, after paying for these seats I can't afford to eat or keep a roof over my head..."

"What happeaned to rich and desperate?"

"Now I'm just desperate."

"I think you're trying to make me feel guilty."

He leaned over, dropping his voice to a whisper meant only for her. "You bet I am. Woman, I want you to feel guilty...and beholden, and all those other wonderful things that will make it easier for me to have my way with you later."

His words sent a responsive vibration through her. "You had a chance to have your way with me the other night," she whispered back, "and you passed it up."

"Postponed it. I think they call it taking a rain check."

"Too bad it's not raining out tonight."

"The night," he informed her with a resurgence of the smug grin she was developing a fatal weakness for, "isn't over yet."

Soon after the lights dimmed and the curtain rose, Kalı wished the night would never be over. It seemed as magical to her as the world of *The Nutcracker* and the Prince and the Sugarplum Fairy. Sitting beside a mesmerized Sandy, Kali saw the battle of the toy soldiers and the mice and the enchanted Kingdom of Sweets as if for the first time. Finally the curtain fell on the magnificent set with its rainbow of candy colors. When the cast had taken its final bow, Sandy turned to first Kali, then Jesse, her eyes wonder filled, expressing all she couldn't or wouldn't say with words.

After the ballet, they went to the Tavern on the Green in the middle of Central Park. The dazzling array of white lights outside and the kaleidoscope of dancing reflections provided by the restaurant's many mirrors and stained-glass windows perpetuated the evening's magical spell.

Sandy, Kali judged from her quick smile and animated expression, was thoroughly enchanted...with the ballet and the night and perhaps especially with the man who had made it all happen. The man who added the cherry from the top of his hot-fudge sundae to the mountain of whipped cream atop hers, and who promised to take her horseback riding on her Christmas vacation. Jesse had made a conquest for life.

Kali told him so after they returned an exhausted but happy Sandy to her parents.

"I was worried she might resist being with someone new, but you were wonderful." Her tone hummed with pride.

"Thanks," he responded dryly. "You don't have to sound so surprised."

"Well, I guess I am, a little. I didn't expect you to be nearly so patient...or so adept at dealing with someone with Sandy's handicap."

He shrugged awkwardly. "I have to admit I was a little surprised myself when I found out how you spend your Monday nights." They had picked up the Jaguar before taking Sandy home; after shifting into a cruising gear, he reached for Kali's hand. "Even when you told me you used the clown costume for volunteer work, I figured your involvement was probably ninety-nine percent publicity and hype and one percent work."

"Thanks a lot." She mimicked his earlier tone.

Chuckling, Jesse lifted her hand to his mouth for a lingering kiss that left her tingling and hungry. "I was wrong and...I'm sorry."

"You're getting very good at saying that."

"I seem to be getting lots of practice," he grumbled playfully, then shot her a glance that was unabashedly curious. "So tell me how you began working with Sandy."

Kali explained how she'd planned to be a special-education teacher before being "discovered" and had decided shortly after arriving in the city to put what she'd learned to use by helping with a variety of volunteer programs.

"It wasn't strictly a magnanimous move," she finished with a slightly self-derisive chuckle. "It was a good way to fill all the lonely weekends."

"I can't imagine anyone as beautiful as you ever having to be lonely."

"How you look has nothing to do with it. Sometimes I felt loneliest when I wasn't alone."

His gaze jerked from the road in surprise; he stared at her for long seconds before nodding. "I think I know what you mean."

For those few seconds Kali felt their communion deepen. Gradually they seemed to be connecting on a level more profound than speech or intellect, through some emotional channel she had never before explored. She moved her hand inside his so their fingers were laced and his warm palm was pressed tightly to hers.

"Tell me about Sandy," he urged in an easy tone that expanded the fragile mood rather than shattering it.

"I started working with her a little over a year ago. According to the introductory reports I read, she began to display all the classic signs of infantile autism when she was about two years old."

"Classic signs," Jesse repeated, his brow furrowed in thought. "You mean like rocking back and forth? Or concentrating on one object for a long time?"

Kali's eyebrows shot up in surprise. "That's right. By the time I met her she'd already progressed past most of that, but Jenny—her mother—has told me that Sandy would sit on the floor for hours spinning a pie plate on its side. Over and over while she stared as if transfixed."

"What sort of work do you do with her?"

"Play the piano, work on jigsaw puzzles, take her places...like tonight. Anything that will draw her out from behind that veil of self-absorption. Basically my role is to help build her self-confidence and provide social reinforcement other than that offered by her family or therapist...some real contact with the world outside."

Jesse nodded. "How's she doing?"

"Better since Jenny and Stan managed to get her into an individualized program run by the state. We know she can read, and she can play the piano by ear. Her perception of spaces and angles is amazing...she can finish half a puzzle while I'm still sorting the pieces into groups by color." Kali trailed off as she caught the racing note of excitement in her voice. "I guess I sound like a boasting parent."

"You have a right to boast. Not many people would have the patience to help someone who never responds."

"But she does respond," Kali cried. "You saw her tonight...she was thrilled and grateful. She's expressing her emotions more and more all the time, and she spends less and less time in that aloof, self-focused mood. She just doesn't...talk."

"Will she? Isn't it possible that a breakthrough could happen spontaneously? Someday she could just start talking?"

Kali nodded, feeling both the hope and wonder that thoughts of Sandy often incited. "The experts say anything is possible. There's been some speculation that her condition is linked to a severe ear infection she suffered as an infant. The drugs used to treat the infection sent her into severe dehydration."

"You mean there could be a neurological reason for her not speaking."

"That's one theory. If so, there might someday be something the doctors can do about it. Or, as you just said, she might have a breakthrough. For now her therapist seems to think it best to simply praise and reward all the positive things she is learning and doing." She tilted her head to the side, regarding him quizzically. "How do you know so much about autism, anyway? Most people don't even know what it is."

Jesse glanced out his side window at a passing car, then shrugged. "I took a few special-ed courses in college myself."

"Were you planning on teaching?"

"No."

"Well, those few courses really paid off tonight—you won Sandy's heart."

He braked for a red light and turned to face her. "It's your heart I'm interested in winning, Kali."

Kali ran her tongue over suddenly dry lips. The anticipation that had been simmering all evening exploded, and she was filled with the unwavering certainty of a woman who has found everything she's been searching for.

"Then you're in luck—it's yours, Jesse."

She was vaguely aware of a light turning from red to green and of horns blasting impatiently. She was intensely aware of the tiny crinkle lines at the sides of Jesse's eyes as he broke into a slow smile, and of the spicy drift of his after-shave and of the way his chest rose and fell in perfect cadence with her thundering heart.

"Look out there, Kali," he said softly, nodding in the direction of the front windshield. His voice was tinged with the same passion she saw in his expression. "It's raining after all."

She darted a glance out the window at the puffs of white that tumbled freely from the heavens, to be scattered like wind-tossed diamonds before the car headlights.

"You idiot," she chided lightly. "That happens to be snow."

Snow. Her joyous mood crumbled as she remembered the weather forecast: a heavy snowfall tonight could mean a delay in air traffic on Christmas Eve. And a delay getting away, coupled with the storm being forecast for the Midwest on Christmas day, meant she would be spending the holiday here in the city. Without her family, and without Jesse.

Seeing the look on her face, Jesse reached over to pull her closer.

"Oh, love," he whispered against her lips as his mouth found hers with all the lightness of the silently falling snow. "Don't worry about the snow, or whether or not planes are flying to North Dakota...I just want you to come home with me. Please."

Kali didn't even pause. She saw no need to weigh the momentous implications of her answer. The urging of her heart was too strong, too pure to be second-guessed.

"I want to go home with you, Jesse." Her wide-set blue eyes were ablaze with a longing that was new and over-powering. "Oh, Jesse, I want *you*."

Jesse's heart seemed to constrict wildly, first with surprise, then with sheer elation.

Of course she had misunderstood what he was suggesting. Her heart-lifting candor in announcing that she wanted him—*wanted* him—told him that she thought he was asking her to come home with him for the night, not home to Rhode Island to spend Christmas with his family. He could have her...now...tonight. He could have all the warmth and sweetness he'd been dreaming about for weeks now.

The familiar urgency inside his body clamored for him to do just that, to disregard the misunderstood question and act on the answer she'd freely given. For it had been freely given; this time he'd exerted no influence with his words or his body. Kali was ready for them to make love. He could see that in the excited flutter of her long lashes and the awkward, anxious way she was waiting for him to say something.

But despite all the surface signals that screamed surrender, her posture reflected an underlying tenseness and something more...vulnerability. And suddenly Jesse knew that he didn't want to be intimate with Kali on a night when she might be seeking nothing more than a warm buffer against the chill of spending Christmas alone.

He didn't want it that way for him or for Kali, who would probably fret afterward that she'd made an impulsive mistake. He wanted nothing, no doubts or regrets or uncertainties, to mar their love for each other. The notion that he loved this woman, who sat trembling expectantly in his arms, came a lot easier this time. And somewhere deep inside him a new feeling of protectiveness struggled to the surface.

Jesse leaned forward and traced the fascinating curve of her mouth with his tongue, stalling, searching for a way to protect her sensitivity and make it clear that this was a clarification, not a rejection.

"Kali," he ventured finally, his deep voice shaded with tender amusement and a fervent need not to hurt her. "I'm afraid I can sometimes be as klutzy with words as I am on a dance floor. It wasn't my bed I was trying to lure you home to this time, love. It was to meet my mother."

8

KALI SMILED AT him in the shadowy interior of the car, heedless of the stream of angry drivers veering around them. The revelation was an unexpected bonus. It thrilled her and enriched the feeling of certainty flowing hotly through her veins. It didn't for one instant sway her from her purpose.

There would be time later to accept his invitation and tell him now much it meant to have him ask her. This moment was for something much more important, something long overdue, and Kali reached out to Jesse with her eyes and her hands to tell him so.

"So it's home to your mother, not to your bed," she mused in a soft echo of his explanation. "Are you sure the two are mutually exclusive?"

Jesse's eyes narrowed. "Are you saying..."

"I think I've already said it, Jesse. Quite plainly, too." She leaned closer and brushed her lips across his in a slow, intentionally tantalizing invitation. "I want you to make love to me...now...tonight."

He drew a deep breath and let it out roughly. "Oh, God, that's all I want to do, Kali, all I've been able to think about for weeks now."

"Then at the risk of sounding pushy, why are we still sitting here?"

"I think half the city is asking itself that same question—only not nearly as politely." With a wry grin he shifted the car into gear and eased into the line of glaring drivers.

The drive to Kali's apartment took only minutes. Perfect minutes filled with a heady sense of anticipation and mounting excitement. She was hardly aware of leaving the car or of the elevator ride to the fourteenth floor. She seemed to be moving in some magical, effortless way, floating and melting at once, and Kali knew the magic emanated from the man whose sure steps echoed her own, whose arm felt strong and warm and oh so right riding the curve of her hip.

Only when the stepped into her living room and Jesse began to peel the velvet cape from her shoulders did a hint of awkwardness intrude. To be swept away in a moment of passion was one thing; to consciously surrender to passion was something quite different, and for Kali, uncharted territory.

Pressed tightly against him, vividly aware of the urgency of his desire, she could feel the tension in her smile. "Would you like a glass of wine first—I mean, would you like a glass of wine? Or something?"

Jesse's smile was calming, touched with tender amusement and the unspoken promise to take all the time she needed. "I don't need wine, Kali," he said quietly, "or anything else. All I need tonight is you. And that I need very badly. But not enough to rush you through this, love. We have all night."

He kissed her temple, the slant of her jaw and finally brought the damp heat of his mouth close to hers. Kali expected him to give her an impassioned kiss, but the contact was whisper light, and she was unconsciously yearning toward him when he pulled her head to his shoulder and cradled her there. Her awkwardness ebbed. The man was magic, pure magic.

He lifted her hand to his mouth and ran his tongue lightly over the pads of her fingers. "You like that," he remarked lightly when she shivered in response. "I'm going to find out all the other kinds of touches and strokes you like, too, Kali, because I have a feeling even you don't know what kind of loving you like best."

Kali's teeth closed over her bottom lip. He was right, she realized as her thoughts turned back to Rick and that weekend right after she'd moved to New York, when he had come to visit her. He had been glum...hurt and angry with her for leaving him behind. Kali had been nervous and eager to convince him and herself that she was still the same person she'd always been. The entire visit was a disaster, especially her last-ditch effort to relieve the strained, awkward atmosphere by going to bed with him. For Kali, that had been a clumsy, joyless initiation into physical love.

It was then that she had vowed never to make love to anyone unless the feeling was exactly that...love. She had stood her ground ever since against accusations that she was frigid, or worse. It had never occurred to her to wonder if her lack of experience had been part of the problem that first time, to wonder if she would even be a satisfactory lover. She wondered now.

"I guess my experience is a little..." She shrugged, fighting the urge to avert her eyes. "Limited."

"Are you trying to tell me you're a virgin?"

She shook her head hastily, astonished that he would think her that inexperienced. "There was one other time...a man I used to—"

"Shh." His fingers fell softly against her lips, stilling her halting explanation. "It doesn't matter, Kali. All that matters is that we're together now, and that you're heart is pounding just as hard as mine is."

"Harder, I think."

"Let's see." His eyes flared, more silver now than green as he placed his palm over her heart. The velvet of her dress might as well have been gossamer. His touch caused a dipping sensation in her stomach, and the tips of her breasts hardened. If her heart hadn't been throbbing in overdrive, it was now. Jesse smiled in full, sensuous recognition. "I think maybe you're right."

"And I think you're very accomplished at this. When we first walked in here I was feeling a little nervous," she admitted with a shrug.

His fingers moved on her breast. "And now?"

"And now I feel impatient."

"That makes two of us."

Kali felt the gruff words, tasted them as he bent his head and took her lips, this time with the demanding passion she had expected earlier. It devoured all resistance, so that Kali wondered why she'd ever been foolish enough to resist Jesse in the first place. It didn't matter what might happen in the future. He was right. All that mattered was that they were together now, and that he made her happy. He made her glow. More than that, he made her burn in a way she never had before.

His hands swept along her spine as his tongue caressed the inside of her mouth insistently. Kali arched against him as his palms cupped her hips and urged her closer. Desire pulsed inside her. The touch of his hands, rolling smoothly over the velvet, became as much torture as pleasure. She trembled to have those hands on her bare skin, yearned to have her hands on him.

Kali could feel the ferocity of his need with each rocking movement of his hips. The blatantly masculine power of him plumbed some primitive, untapped reservoir of response, appealing to everything in her that was woman.

She wanted to ease his need, as well as her own, which threatened to storm out of control as his fingers swirled from her hips to her breast, then back, along her thighs and between. His head dipped, and his teeth grated sensually along her throat. Pleasure ripped through Kali. She shivered and trembled in his arms, letting the strength of his hard frame take her weight.

"I think I've discovered something else you like." His low-pitched voice was in itself a caress.

"I think I've discovered I like everything you do."

She bit her lip as he laughed softly and moved her hair aside to trace the curve of her ear with his tongue. The contact sent an unfamiliar thread of sensation zigzagging to the pit of her stomach, making everything inside melt and drizzle toward the spot where his hand was pressed very low on her belly. Her knees bent; her fingers curled into his shoulders, clinging to the smooth fabric of his jacket.

"Jesse, when you do that it makes it hard for me to stand up."

"I'm glad, because I'd much rather do it with you lying in my arms." He lifted her easily off the floor and held her close to his chest, his expression a heated blend of tenderness and impatience. "The sofa or your bed?"

She measured the narrow sofa against his broad shoulders and smiled. "The bed, I think. That way."

He started down the hall, stepping into her pale-toned room and nudging the door partially closed behind them with his shoulder. Once he had placed her in the center of the bed, the ivory satin coverlet felt cool against her skin. Kali thought that sensation probably had more to do with her own overheated state than anything else. A sliver of light from the other room cast Jesse's silhouette on the wall as he stripped off his jacket and tie. He moved to the bed, and for a moment just stood there, gazing down on her, his pleasure easy to read even in the shadows. Kali's heart thumped wildly in response.

"You're beautiful," he said simply, one knee denting the mattress beside her. "I want this to last forever."

"Me, too. I've never felt this way before... Oh, Jesse, I want so much to please you."

"You will, Kali," he murmured against her hair. "Just loving you will please me." He rubbed his cheek against the strands of pale gold silk. "And I want to be gentle with you...as if it was the first time. In some ways it will be...for both of us." He levered up briefly to look at her, his eyes ablaze with passion and promises. "I've never made love to a woman I was in love with before."

Then he was kissing her again, and Kali was wrapping her arms around him, pulling him closer, thrilling to the yearning, rocking motion of his hips against hers. His body shifted so that one muscular thigh lay between hers, the pressure light and tantalizing. His hands swept from her hair to her shoulders.

"Mmm, what is this called?" he asked distractedly, fingering the soft fabric of her dress.

"Velvet," whispered Kali, shaken by the erotic sensations he was once more arousing with the flick of his tongue along the inner paths of her ear.

"It feels almost as good as you do." He reached beneath her and lowered the zipper to her waist, loosening the bodice enough to permit the free roving of his fingers. They moved slowly over her skin, wandering down to her ribs, then back up by tantalizing fractions of an inch until the palm of his hand grazed the full undercurve of her breast. Kali sucked in her breath sharply, making her swell against him, eliciting a rough chuckle of delight from Jesse that tickled her neck.

Twisting beneath him, Kali clutched at the back of his shirt, tugging it free of his slacks, suddenly desperate to touch him without the buffer of constricting fabric. Jesse lifted up just enough so that she could ride his shirt higher, until the heated flesh of his bare chest was pressed to hers. The pounding of his heart was hard and heavy, and the muscles of his back tensed and rippled in response to the tentative strokes of her fingers. The flesh-and-blood evidence of his susceptibility to her touch filled Kali with awe, and an odd feeling of power that fueled her desire.

The feeling mounted as his hips continued to move against her in a steady, pulsing contact that stirred her awakened senses. Her head fell to the side, permitting his lips access for nibbling meanderings. When he raked his teeth gently along the side of her throat, she whispered his name, a plea and a command mingled in the husky depths of her voice.

Still his fingers played just beneath her breasts, until aching with longing to have him touch her, Kali circled his wrist and dragged his hand in a slow, steady line to one pink-hued tip. Jesse's breath dragged from him in a jagged sigh as his fingers began an obedient, circling caress of her aroused nipple.

"I take back what I said a minute ago," he breathed, his lips pressed close to her ear. "Velvet doesn't even come close. I've never felt anything so soft."

Kali turned her head, bringing her mouth to his, and lifted her hands to frame his face and hold him steady for her kiss. Jesse was a willing captive. His lips fell open at the first urging of her tongue. Kali swept across their hot, moist surface with delicate strokes. Weeks of his sometimes tender, sometimes love-potion-strong kisses had made her an expert at this art, and now she applied all she had learned to the task of bringing him pleasure. She licked at the corners, then thrust past his lips to relearn the mixture of rough and sleek textures inside.

Jesse, she discovered quickly and with slightly hazy amazement, brought no macho preconceptions to his lovemaking. As she deepened the kiss provocatively, he rolled to his side, permitting her greater control of the pressure and tempo. Kali thrilled to the challenge, letting her tongue move inside him in long, rhythmic strokes that came as naturally to her as the breath that mingled with his in a sweet, heated rush.

Drawing back so that their mouths were barely touching, she glided her passion-slick lips back and forth across his; the two met as softly as shadows sliding together in the moonlight. The sensation unleashed by the light contact was electric and totally unexpected, sending a tremor racing through her body.

"You're playing with fire, love," Jesse warned softly, moving his thumb back and forth across her nipple in slow, hypnotic strokes.

Kali pressed her lips to the side of his neck, tasting the heat and salt of his flesh.

"Fire," she echoed in a voice heavy with passion. "I thought it was beginning to feel a little. . .warm in here."

His deep chuckle danced across her cheek. "I think I know just the cure for that."

"But I don't want to be cured," she protested, then felt his hands tugging her dress lower, easing it over her hips and thighs, and her complaint melted into a smile.

The dress drifted to the chair beside the bed as his fingers moved to her waist and slipped between her tingling flesh and her pantyhose. A heartbeat later they, along with her lace slip and panties, had been slipped off in one alarmingly expert swoop.

"You're very good at that," Kali managed to say between gulps as he touched every inch of her with eyes that were hungry and adoring.

"It's not all that difficult." Jesse smiled, a reassuring flash of white teeth beneath an alluringly slanted mustache. His fingers closed over hers, carrying them to his belt buckle. "Here, try it for yourself."

As soon as his hands fell away, hers skittered higher, latching haphazardly onto the top button of his shirt.

"Maybe I'll just start here and sort of...work my way down," she explained, seeing the teasing glint in his eye.

After the first button, her maneuvering came easily. Lured on by the sight of his broad chest with its dark arrow of soft, curling hair, her fingers moved eagerly. She dragged the shirt off his shoulders and arms, baring a magnificent arrangement of sculptured muscles and enticing hollows.

With a fresh surge of desire, she settled her fingers over his buckle and worked it open, then dealt with the snap and zipper and began to slide the slacks over the lean, fascinatingly male terrain of his hips and legs. Even with Jesse twisting and lifting to help, she had to kneel to finish the job. When she had his pants completely off, she ran her gaze over him, feeling it heat from shy to hungry as it caressed the ridges and angles of his body. He was excitingly virile, so close to her image of masculine perfection.

Kali was mesmerized, excitement throbbing within as the hint of light played over his skin, burnishing it with a golden glow. Jesse lay still under her breathless perusal, making a soft, yearning sound only when she bent to brush moist kisses along the border where white underwear met taut, bronze flesh. Kali felt the powerful muscles there spasm beneath the light touch of her lips, and that spurred her on.

Slowly, feeling the imprint of her lover's eyes like a caress, she slipped her fingers beneath the elastic waistband of his shorts and began to strip them off. In the process her fingers brushed against his full erection. The sensation of silk and fire came as a shock, and Kali jerked her gaze up to find Jesse moaning, his complexion a dull red, moisture beading on his body. He was like something untamed, and her blood surged in a wild blending of passion and alarm.

It was a potent combination, she discovered as he grasped her about the waist and twisted her flat on her back beneath him. The pressure of his hips against hers was grinding, insistent, but the hands sweeping from her breasts to her hips and thighs were gentle, and his murmured, disjointed phrases were love soft, riddled with words of praise and demand.

As his rough-tipped fingers scorched a path across the sensitized skin of her belly, time turned into a string of slow-moving moments, unconnected to all that had gone before in their lives and all that would come after. There was only Jesse, and Kali, and the fierce, flaming desire that fused their souls and made their bodies strain for the same privilege.

Her lips opened deeply beneath Jesse's kiss as his fingers coasted lower, feathering the soft curls that sheltered her femininity. Even before he touched her Kali sensed a growing tautness. The pressure built while everything inside her melted, running in a warm, honeyed flow toward the part of her that throbbed in sweet anticipation.

She was past being ready; she was burning up with the fire he patiently stoked higher. Still she gasped in surprise at the first warm touch of his fingers—the first time any man had touched her that way. Her fingers clenched around the resilient curve of his shoulder, tears dampening her cheeks as with tenderness and patience he guided her into a whole new dimension of intimacy, touching her with his hands and mouth in ways even her most erotic fantasies had never approached.

She was still reeling from the avalanche of new sensations his skilled touch had created when he shifted on top of her, his face darkly handsome and tight with desire. His hands bracketed her hips firmly.

"Kali, love, open your legs for me...please." His voice was husky, the words scattered between kisses pressed against her parted lips. "A little bit more...ah, that's it...that's...perfect."

He fitted himself into the place she had made for him between her parted thighs and breathed, "Wrap your legs around me."

Kali obeyed. Then, slowly, murmuring a constant stream of reassurance, he joined their bodies. Kali felt the hot, sliding union in every pore, every trembling nerve, with heightened sensitivity that had her tottering on the edge of control. Jesse seemed to be fighting the same battle. He held himself stock still above her, eyes squeezed shut, until she felt some of the tenseness seeping from him, starting at the nape of his neck.

When his breathing had steadied, he lifted his head to smile down at her, his eyes as dark as midnight at sea. "Thank you for not moving...for a minute there I came pretty close to falling short of both of our expectations."

Kali shook her head in fervent denial. "You've already surpassed all mine," she whispered.

Jesse groaned harshly and lowered his mouth to her breast, tugging and lapping it to fuller arousal as he at last began to move inside her. His strokes were deep and slow, as smooth as velvet and as powerful as the surge of a riptide. Kali felt herself being transformed into a sea of pulsing sensations, shimmering, rushing toward the fulfillment only she and Jesse could find together.

And she was moving with him, haltingly at first, until his gentle hands taught her the rhythm of passion and roused the cavewoman hiding deep inside her. Slowly he carried her higher. Again and again Kali arched against him and with him, while her gaze was held prisoner by the hypnotic intensity of his.

With each thrust, each soft moan of desire, she felt that he probed deeper, that his eyes saw more clearly and further into her soul than even she had dared to explore before now. But she didn't look away...she didn't want to look away, for the process of exposure and discovery worked both ways. She was bewitched by the Jesse she saw through the windows of his passion-bright eyes.

"God, Kali, you feel good." His teeth were clenched, his expression intense, the tempo of his movements relentless, constantly strengthening the current of sensuality bubbling through her.

Together their breathing became quick and shallow, and together their movements grew more urgent. When Jesse's body finally tautened and shuddered with completion, he took Kali with him into a world of splendor and sensation that was older than time and newer than tomorrow's sunrise.

It was a long, silent while later when he got up to tug the covers from beneath her sleepy, protesting body, then stretched out beside her beneath the welcome warmth. His hand settled comfortably on her hip. The curling hairs covering his chest brushed her breasts. One hard thigh felt very much at home between hers.

Eyes glinting with lazy satisfaction, he threaded his fingers through the gold of her hair and smiled like a man who had it all.

THICK, SNOW-FILLED CLOUDS hung outside the window of the commuter plane, preventing Kali from catching even a glimpse of the New England landscape below. With a sigh she turned away and once more closed her eyes, wishing the fifty-minute flight from New York to the airport near Jesse's Cumberland, Rhode Island, home was at least several hours longer. She could use the recovery time.

Last night had been gloriously sleepless—and she didn't regret one second of it. Like some potent brand of magic, Jesse's loving had swept all doubts and misgivings from her mind. She had climbed from the love-tousled bed exhausted but happy. The morning was spent rushing around the city, dropping off the video game that was her Christmas present to Sandy and her family, then the specially ordered copy of a rare old Beatles album that Glen had been combing record shops for for months. After that she had hustled from Macy's to the small, homemade-candy shop a few blocks from her apartment in a burst of last-minute shopping for the McPherson's. Also, she had to choose a few backups for the special gift she wasn't sure was going to please Jesse at all.

Then there had been an emotional phone call to North Dakota. Her parents were disappointed that she wouldn't be arriving home that afternoon as planned, but not really surprised. They had been monitoring the weather forecasts at their end and understood that her chances of ending up snowbound either coming or going were too great to risk. They did promise to keep the tree up and all her presents under it until she could make it home for a few days in early January. They made her promise, as well, that she would be careful—very careful—around this Jesse whom she'd never mentioned a word about in any of her letters, and who all of a sudden was friendly enough to bring her home with him for Christmas.

Kali hadn't wanted to go into her feelings for Jesse over the telephone, but she did hint that he was special...very special. That only seemed to fuel their concern. She was warned to remember, in her mother's words, that smooth-talking men were a dime a dozen, and all that glitters is not gold. Her father, with a catch in his voice, simply told her to have a Merry Christmas and not worry about calories for once in her life. Will, the only one of her brothers around when she called, displayed a quite belligerent attitude toward the man who was giving his sister such a rush thousands of miles away from where he could keep an eye on things. When he found out that her Jesse was *the* Jesse McPherson, Kali noted with amusement that she quickly went from being a troublesome sister to a valuable asset. She was expected to secure inside information on the world of professional hockey.

The desire for a nap after all that running around wasn't the only reason Kali wished the plane ride would take longer. Suddenly she felt as if she were sixteen again and on her way to meet her boyfriend's parents for the first time. Her palms were sweaty, and she felt compelled to smooth her hair over and over again. There was no hiding her nervousness. Jesse, predictably, found her discomfiture a perfect target for his teasing. He eyed her critically, pretending to think long and hard when she asked him for the third time if he was sure her jacquard-style wrap sweater and slate-blue slacks looked all right.

"Actually," he announced, deadpan, "I like you better in your plaid robe."

"I mean honestly."

"Believe me, that was honest." He chuckled at her frustrated glare and mused softly, "I wonder if you were ever this concerned before about what I thought of the way you look."

"Of course not. With you I've always had more pressing things to fret about."

"Such as?"

"Oh, such as wondering when—if ever—you would finally get around to making love with me."

Jesse's mouth gaped in a satisfyingly stunned way. "You're kidding."

"No," Kali lied. "You have to admit you have been a little...slow."

"Slow?" he demanded in the loudest, most outraged whisper she'd ever heard. "Is that what they call being a gentleman these days? Being slow?"

Kali executed her most eloquent shrug. "It was a little surprising. I mean with your wild reputation and all, but I suppose what my mother always says is true."

"Exactly what does she say?"

Kali marveled that he could speak so clearly through clenched teeth. "You know, that you can't tell a book by its cover."

He watched her thoughtfully for a moment, and when he spoke again the familiar amusement was back in his voice. "My mother had some different advice for me. She always said you should be careful that you want what you ask for because you just might get it."

"Promises, promises," Kali taunted softly, then felt the advantage of the game shift as his hand came down heavily on her thigh.

"Care to put your money where your mouth is?"

The quiet challenge and the predatory look he sent with it scattered her arsenal of witty retorts. "Of course not," she mumbled with a stab at looking haughty. "I would never bet on such a thing."

"I would." The very proper-looking man in the seat next to Jesse, who had seemed so engrossed in his news magazine, lifted his head as he spoke. Behind horn-rimmed glasses his eyes twinkled, and the sides of his mouth twitched with barely restrained laughter. "Ten dollars says the little lady's got more spunk than your whole team."

The little lady might have spunk, but she didn't have enough interest in the technical aspects of hockey to participate in the ensuing discussion between Jesse and their seatmate. He'd recognized Jesse as the star of his favorite team when he'd boarded and had just been waiting for a chance to introduce himself. They were almost ready to land when he finally excused himself, letting Jesse turn back to Kali.

"Are you still worried?" he asked.

"Of course not. I'm just grinding the enamel off my teeth to pass the time."

He chuckled, a rich, masculine sound that momentarily distracted Kali from her panicky visions of all that could go wrong over the next two days. She wasn't usually this anxious about the impression she made on others, but there was nothing usual or ordinary about her feelings for Jesse. She wanted the family that meant so much to him to like her.

"You really are nervous," he said incredulously, enclosing her damp-palmed hand in his warm, dry one. "I shouldn't have teased you before."

"That's okay. I shouldn't have cast aspersions on your manhood."

His mustache twitched. "My manhood will survive."

"But will I?" she fretted. "Tell me again—"

"You look beautiful."

"I was going to say tell me about your family."

"I already did."

"Oh, you told me that mother is a housewife and proud of it, and that your dad is a teacher. I know you have two sisters and a brother, but what are they all like?"

Jesse brushed the perpetually uncooperative wave of hair back from his forehead. "They're just an ordinary family, who live in a big, ordinary old house, and celebrate Christmas in a very ordinary way." He hesitated, then added, "With one small exception. I didn't tell you about Danny."

"Your brother?"

Jesse nodded, and Kali thought the hand holding hers tensed a little as he began to speak.

"Danny is retarded, Kali...mildly retarded is the technical diagnosis. His supply of oxygen was cut off for several minutes during his birth and..."

He trailed off to watch her in a wary, guarded way, looking for signs—of what Kali wasn't sure. Shock? Revulsion? Apparently he detected nothing discouraging in her calm, interested expression, so he continued.

"He's a great kid, Kali." He flashed a smile and shrugged. "Kid...he's twenty-one now and nearly as tall as I am. He even has a job of his own through a state-run program, but it's still hard not to think of him as a kid. He's so open and trusting, and he has more energy and enthusiasm than anyone I know."

Kali nodded. "I know what you mean. I worked with several retarded children before I got involved with Sandy, and so many times I found that I was learning from them...learning to be sensitive, and to slow down and appreciate the small, everyday things most people never even notice."

"I should have known you'd feel this way, that you would understand." He shook his head, his voice laden with self-recrimination. "But I was afraid. That's why I didn't ask you to come home with me when you first mentioned you might end up spending Christmas alone. I wanted to."

"When you said you had to go home, snow or no snow, I couldn't help wondering if maybe there was someone waiting for you at home...a woman who didn't have a crazy job you disapproved of, and who would always be around when you needed her."

"The only one I have to get home for is Danny. He really looks forward to the whole family being together for Christmas. I couldn't let him down, Kali—not even for you."

"I'm glad. And I think I understand why you didn't tell me about Danny before this. At first I felt the same way about having you meet Sandy. I was afraid you'd be put off by the fact that she's disabled."

"I guess we have a lot to learn about each other."

"Maybe not so much. Maybe we should just stop looking for flaws in each other and accept that we've known from the start—that we're alike in a lot of ways."

"But not, thank God, in a way that counts just as much."

If she hadn't picked up on the innuendo in his lazy declaration, the scorching look in his dark eyes would have told her exactly which difference Jesse had on his mind.

He leaned closer and took her mouth in a kiss that was long and hungry and unleashed pleasure that washed through Kali like a tidal wave. They both pulled back reluctantly when their chatty friend slipped once more into his seat. The flight attendant was instructing passengers to fasten their seat belts for landing at Theodore F. Green Airport, where the temperature was a snowy twenty-four degrees.

The trepidation that had been simmering inside Kali since the moment she'd accepted Jesse's invitation reached a palpitating crescendo as they approached the heavy doors separating the boarding ramp from the main airport.

"Jesse, do you think your whole family will be here to meet you?" Kali asked, not sure whether she'd rather meet them en masse or one at a time.

"I don't know."

"Well, do they usually all come?" she pressed a trifle impatiently.

"No." Grinning broadly, he swung her carryon to his other shoulder and circled her shoulders with his free arm.

"But then I've never given them any incentive to by bringing a woman home with me, either."

The fresh burst of panic brought on by that little revelation had no time to take root. They were barely through the swinging doors when Jesse was swallowed up by a trio of very happy people. Kali stood politely to one side, observing the unrestrained warmth that flowed between these people...a bittersweet reminder of her own family.

Mr. McPherson was tall and trim, and one look at him told Kali which parent Jesse favored. The older man's eyes were green and expressive, rimmed with thick black lashes. And his hair was as dark and gleaming as his son's, only threaded with silver at the temples, the way Jesse's would be someday. His mother was pretty and blond, a slightly rounder version of the young woman by her side, whom Kali guessed to be Jesse's sister.

After he'd returned their enthusiastic hugs and kisses and shrugged off his mother's pronouncement that he looked tired—and skinny—he drew Kali into the tight circle.

With one arm curled around her waist, he said, "Mom, Dad, this is Kali Spencer, the lady I told you about. Kali, I want you to meet my parents and my sister Kristen."

Despite her racing nerves, Kali heard the untempered note of pride in his voice and was thrilled. Then she was being hugged by Mrs. McPherson and Kristen and having her hand pumped by Jesse's father, amid a flurry of friendly welcomes and excited questions.

"I hope by coming home with Jesse I haven't put a damper on your family's holiday, Mrs. McPherson," Kali said when Jesse and his father had left to fetch their luggage from the circling conveyor belt.

"Put a damper on it?" Kristen responded before her mother had a chance to. "Your being here is the most exciting thing that's happened since the time Danny set the Christmas tree on fire."

"He'd seen a drawing in a book of a tree decorated with real candles," her mother explained, "and he thought he'd surprise us." She hesitated. "Jesse did tell you about Danny?"

"Yes. I can't wait to meet him." Kali noted the slight, visible relaxing of the older woman's facial muscles and was about to reassure her further, but she didn't get a chance.

"He can't wait to meet you, either," Kristen broke in. "In fact, none of us could wait to get a look at the woman who finally snagged—ouch."

Aiming a regretful smile at Kali, Jesse's mother gracefully removed her foot from her daughter's toes.

"As you can see, we're not exactly the most subtle bunch in the world," she said, "but I hope we make up for it in hospitality. And you are welcome, Kali. I'll tell you right up front that I've been concerned for some time that Jesse couldn't seem to find a girl who pleased him for longer than a few weeks. I hope the fact that he brought you home to meet us is a sign that he finally has. From what I've seen so far, I'd say you were well worth waiting for."

The compliment filled Kali with a rich, satisfying warmth. She was still basking in it as the five of them piled into the family station wagon. Before the twenty-minute drive to the rural community of Cumberland was half over, the remnants of her anxiety had vanished. Along with it went most of the homesickness that had probably contributed to her jittery state. If she had to be away from home on Christmas, she couldn't imagine any place she'd rather be than here with Jesse. In fact, in a way that she could feel but couldn't explain, being with Jesse—no matter where—was beginning to feel more and more like home to her.

Danny, and Jesse's other sister, Beth, proved to be as charmingly unaffected as the rest of the family. Beth's hair was darker than her sister's long, blond tresses, but she was just as exuberant and just as eager to hear anything and everything about the life of a professional model. Kali found their interest flattering, so that during the family's traditional Christmas Eve dinner of Rock Cornish hens and baked, stuffed potatoes, she tried to answer all their questions.

But it was Danny who found a special place in her heart. He was nearly as big as his older brother, and just as handsome in a different way. His appeal was gentler, lacking in the raw masculinity that lurked beneath Jesse's lazy smile and permeated his every move. There was no threat of cynicism in Danny's heartwarming grin, and no intent to embarrass in even his most provocative questions.

For instance, he brought the festive group, busily decking the freshly cut cedar tree with ornaments and tinsel, to a dead stop—he asked Kali if she was going to sleep in his bed or Jesse's.

"Well, it has to be one of them," he pressed innocently when the only response he got was the melodic voice of Bing Crosby singing *White Christmas*. "No one else has room."

Mr. McPherson cleared his throat while his daughters fought back chuckles, and Jesse—the rat—held his strategic position behind the tree and unleashed a leer for Kali's eyes only. "Kali will sleep in Jesse's room," Mrs. McPherson said, coming smoothly to the rescue as she strode in from the kitchen with another batch of hot buttered popcorn. "And he, of course, will bunk in with you, Danny. In fact, I probably should have told you that earlier, Kali, in case you wanted to change or anything. Turn left at the top of the stairs, and it's the last room on the left—your bags are already in there."

"Hey, that's great!" crowed Danny, obviously thrilled with the news that Jesse was to share his room. "I had Dad tape *The Bells of Saint Mary's* so I can play it on the VCR in my room, Jesse. Do you want to watch it together later?"

"Do I want to watch it? You don't think I came all the way home just to string cranberries and get blisters sawing down a tree, do you? Of course we'll watch it."

Kali felt pride surge inside her as she listened, and with it wonder and contentment that the essence of Jesse was so close to what she wanted, and so far from what she had first thought. Her happiness was almost too pure to bear as she watched Danny race off to find the treasured videocassette.

Later, long after midnight, she lay in Jesse's bed and heard the sounds of the familiar old movie coming from the next room. She drifted contentedly off to sleep to the muffled melody of "The Bells of Saint Mary's" delivered in five-part harmony by the nuns' chorus, and woke to a world that was not quite dark and not quite light.

Dawn was just outside the window, its pale pink hue a beacon in a room filled with the dark, unfamiliar shadows of sports trophies and fishing gear. Kali's eyes were barely open, still sleep glazed, when she became rivetingly aware that she was not alone.

Twisting on the bed, she discovered Jesse sitting beside her, caressing her with his gaze in a way that sent burning signals through her and jolted her brain fully awake.

"You're in my bed." The announcement was drawled in a dark tone that disturbed her. How sensual a few casual words could be....."I wonder if you have any idea how the thought of you sleeping here arouses me, Kali?"

KALI BARELY HEARD the suggestively shaded question. Her mind was too tangled with other thoughts.

She wondered how long he'd been lounging there watching her sleep. She wondered if he would dare choose this moment, in the middle of a houseful of McPhersons, who might or might not be safely asleep, to do what they both clearly longed to do. Staring into eyes burning into her like lasers, she knew in a flash that he would dare anything.

"Jesse, no," she whispered, more in response to her own thoughts than his question.

"I didn't think so," he replied carelessly. "That's why I had to come in here...to tell you...and to say good morning... and to wish you a Merry Christmas."

He'd dropped his head to scatter light, brushing kisses between his words. A lover's kisses, a lover's desire-edged words. They were a potent, seductive combination, and when he was finished Kali reached up with a small whimper and dragged him back...the rules of etiquette that usually clung to her like a second skin swept away by the force of the yearning he could so easily incite.

She heard him chuckle softly as he let her guide his lips back to hers. For the moment she was the aggressor, which felt wonderful. She framed his face with her palms, loving the morning-rough feel of his cheeks. Her mouth moved over his lightly at first, duplicating all the teasing, tasting, licking moves they'd shared before. Then she pushed her tongue past the easily conquered barrier of his lips to learn the warm, dark secrets beyond. She explored the varied textures of him—the velvet roughness of his tongue and the warm satin of his lips—until her breath ran out. Then, panting, she dipped her head to trace damp circles on the pulse-point throbbing in his throat.

Jesse straightened his arms so the top half of his body was levered above her, his feet still on the floor. He was, she noticed appreciatively, wearing nothing but snug, faded jeans.

Dropping her head back to the pillow, she smiled up at him. "Merry Christmas."

"Is it time to unwrap our presents?" Grinning wickedly, he supported his weight with one arm while he used the other to jerk the sheet and wash-softened patchwork quilt to her waist.

"Ahh," he said in the tone of one who has just made a discovery of earth-shattering importance. "You do sleep in something besides a bed." His fingers looped beneath the straps of her rose satin nightgown, first one, then the other. "It's pretty. Let's take it off."

With the speed and dexterity he applied to everything, Jesse whisked the gown to her waist. His eyes caught fire as he looked at her, and the protest Kali knew she should be uttering stalled somewhere behind the lump in her throat.

"God, Kali, I don't think you've ever looked as beautiful...." He reached out, trailing his finger over her as he spoke. "With your hair all tousled. . .and your skin flushed...your lips red and swollen from my kisses."

His hand dropped to caress her breast, and he gazed in fascination as the tips responded, growing hard at the command of his fingers.

"Do you know," he asked with interest, "that when you're... excited, your nipples are the exact same color as your nightgown, the same color as the sweater you were wearing the night we met."

His words ended on a husky whisper, his mouth so close to her torso that the heat of his breath warmed her nipple. Then his warm lips and tongue were all around her, drawing her inside, teasing, coaxing, sending pleasure shafting in an unwavering path to some private place deep inside her.

He shifted so that he was sprawled on the bed beside her, his free hand drifting over her ribs, playing them gently as one would the ivory keys of a priceless Steinway. His mouth slid to her other breast. Kali's head tossed on the pillow, and her fingers curled into the smooth muscles of his shoulders. Jesse's hand moved lower, coming to rest on her belly, open, fingers spread, branding its imprint onto her skin right through the layers of sheet and blankets.

Kali trembled and felt a responsive shudder pass through the powerful body covering hers...irrefutable evidence that if Jesse had begun this seduction as a game, he was well beyond that point now. For a moment she vacillated, caught between sanity and a fierce hunger to know more of him, to know all of him. Then the spellbinding effect of his tongue was shattered by a loud clang, followed quickly by a hissing sound somewhere near the foot of the bed.

"Jesse, what was that?" she asked, wondering why he hadn't frozen at the sound, as she had.

His words brushed thickly across her skin. "Just the heat coming up through the radiator—one of the pleasures of living in an old house."

"And that?" She heard a definite scratching sound above the hissing. In fact, she was suddenly aware of all sorts of noises. Any one of which, she thought frantically, could be someone coming looking for Jesse.

"That's the branches outside the window," he murmured. "One of the pleasures of living in an old house in the country."

His hand slipped lower, trailing along one thigh, then back up the other to the spot where they met.

"Jesse," Kali began quietly, fighting to sound composed in spite of the fact that everything inside was melting, running in a hot, sweet drizzle to the spot he was caressing with his palm. "You do remember where we are, don't you?"

Jesse groaned, his mouth and hand falling still simultaneously. "Is this a test?"

"No—it's your parents' house."

"So?"

"So we can't make love here...not when someone could wake up any minute and see that you're not in Danny's room and wonder where you are."

"Why? Would it be so wicked?"

The sudden slant of his mustache should definitely have put her on alert. "Yes...not to mention risky."

"Wicked and risky—that's my favorite kind of sex. How about you?"

"I don't know. I've never sampled either, and if you don't mind, I'd rather not start now."

"What if I do mind?" he countered, moving his hips tantalizingly against hers.

Kali sighed. At least his mood had cooled to the teasing one she recognized well. Whether or not that made him any easier to handle was debatable. "Listen, I'm going to try to put this in terms simple enough for even that caveman inside you to grasp—get off me."

"I can't—he says he's having too much fun to leave."

Kali braced her hands against his shoulders and gave a mighty shove, to which Jesse responded by rolling agilely to land on his feet at the side of the bed.

"If you wanted me to get up," he grumbled, watching her pull her nightgown back up, "why didn't you just say so?"

Her pillow was raised and aimed for retaliation when the sound of vigorously jingling bells at the foot of the stairs brought her up short.

"Don't try telling me that's just the heat," she murmured.

Jesse shook his head piteously. "Of course that's not the heat—it's Santa Claus." Sauntering to the door, he added, "I think I'll mosey on downstairs and see what he brought me."

"Are you sure you've been good?" taunted Kali.

"No." He glanced back over his shoulder, flashing her that slanted smile that did strange things to her respiration. "But I could have sworn you thought I was."

The bells, Kali learned when Beth popped into her room a few minutes later, were another McPherson holiday tradition. Her father had used them to wake up the family when they were children, explaining to their wide-eyed delight that they were the sound of Santa's sleigh taking off from the roof. The custom was continued in part for Danny, who approached the holiday with the ambivalent faith of an eight-year-old, and partly, Beth declared firmly, because it wouldn't be Christmas morning without them.

Another tradition, she insisted, was that no one in the family got dressed for the day until they'd all had coffee and opened their presents. Wearing the deep blue velvet robe with ruffles at the neck and cuffs that she'd bought for her trip home, Kali accompanied Beth downstairs.

They found the rest of the family already assembled around the brightly lit Christmas tree. With the exception of Jesse and Danny, who were dressed only slightly more formally in jeans and sweatshirts, they were all in robes. Kali hesitated at the bottom of the stairs while Beth bounded into the living room.

She suddenly felt awkward, as if she were intruding on a time that should be reserved for family only. Taking one look at her, Jesse stood and started toward her, but Danny beat him to her side and planted a quick, enthusiastic kiss on her mouth.

"The mistletoe," he chortled, pointing up to the dark green sprig with white berries festively tied with red ribbon.

"You should have picked a better spot to get cold feet," Jesse added as he nudged his brother aside. "But as long as you're there..."

His kiss was as unhurried as Danny's had been quick, and as intimate as the other had been childlike, a melding of warm lips and the barest hint of tongue. Afterward, Kali opened her eyes just in time to see the smug, satisfied looks flashing wildly among the five McPhersons waiting in the other room.

As soon as they started opening gifts, Kali's momentary sense of strangeness began to fade. The sounds of paper crinkling and ribbons being snapped mixed with the carols issuing softly from the stereo, the same way they always had in her home on Christmas morning. She found herself drawn into the laughter and teasing as easily as if she'd known this family for a long time.

Kristen lifted the lid off a slim, oblong box with a surprised cry that ended in a small frown as she held up a fine, gold chain. "It's beautiful....but it's the one Beth wanted to go with her green blouse. Do you think *someone* put the wrong name on the tag?" she asked, looking straight at her mother.

"Don't look at me. I never make a mistake."

"Could we have that in writing?"

"Quit squabbling. The tag was right—it's from me," Beth said.

"Beth! Why would you give me the chain you wanted?"

"So I'd have it to wear with my green blouse, of course."

"How thoughtful."

"See? Sometimes it is better to give then to receive."

"In that case...open this one next." Kristen handed her sister a box identical to the one still cradled in her lap.

"I can hardly stand the suspense.... Do you suppose jewelry can be exchanged?"

"I don't know," Jesse interjected, "but I sure hope pajamas can be. Mom, every year I tell you I don't wear pajamas."

"And every year I tell you you're going to catch pneumonia."

"I doubt that that's big brother's style."

"That's enough, Beth. Besides," she continued, returning her attention to her smirking elder son, "even if you don't wear them right away, you'll need them if you ever have occasion to go on a honeymoon."

"Mom, a honeymoon is the very last occasion that would call for red-and-white-striped pajamas.

"What color *would* you wear?" his younger sister demanded saucily.

"Beth, why don't you just open your own presents?"

"I am. Oh, Kali—Tatiana! It smells gorgeous—thank you."

"You're welcome, Beth."

Jesse scowled at Kali. "You gave her my perfume?"

Beth giggled. "Don't worry, Jesse, I'll share it with you."

"I meant it's the perfume I like on Kali."

"I think you'd like Eau de Skunk on Kali."

Kali hurriedly lifted the top from the first of several boxes from Jesse and peeled away the tissue to reveal a designer silk scarf in a deep shade of rose. "Jesse, thank you. I love it."

"I'm glad," he responded, his voice soft and deep. "It's the exact same shade as..." From clear across the room, his eyes glittered in a way that sent warmth radiating to her cheeks. "The sweater you were wearing the night we met."

Kali breathed a sigh of relief at his discretion. "It's beautiful—I mean, they're beautiful," she added as she noticed another scarf beneath the first, this one a clear, china blue.

"That one's the same color as your eyes, "Jesse explained. "And the next one is the color of that dress you wore to the ballet."

"Did he say ballet?" That was Kristen.

There was a quiet chorus of amused chuckles, which he ignored with regal detachment.

"The others match the blouse you had on the day you came to watch me practice and your red parka. The white one I just threw in because I liked it."

Kali looked up from the box holding a small fortune in scarves to Jesse's smiling face. He seemed unconcerned about presenting her with such an unabashedly romantic gift in front of his whole family, and about the conclusions they were bound to draw from his openness. She knew from the expressions on the faces around her, and because she knew Jesse, that he wasn't given to such public displays of affection. In her throat a tight, hard lump formed, making her words come out haltingly.

"It's a wonderful gift, Jesse. It makes me feel sort of bad that I bought you the last thing in the world you want."

Jesse was intrigued by that. He poked around in his pile of gifts and held up the one containing the leather gloves she'd bought to match his flight jacket. "This?"

Kali shook her head.

"This?" He repeated, hoisting the box containing the small, comical statue of a cavemen beating his chest that she hadn't been able to resist buying when she'd seen it in a shop window. On the base it read, "Nobody told me there'd be days like this."

"Not that one," she said. "Try the big, square box with the silver bow."

He lifted it onto the table in front of him and quickly tore off the paper and lid. The irritated, scowling protest Kali fully expected did not materialize. Instead he gazed at her with a thoughtful, searching expression as he reached in and extracted the helmet bearing the Bandits' colors and insignia.

"Alleluia!" his mother exclaimed the instant she saw it, breaking the silence that had hovered over the unveiling.

His father nodded, smiling broadly. "I'll second that."

"Thank you," Jesse said to Kali. He even smiled, a droll twist of his mustache that she found entrancing. "But you were wrong—I wouldn't say it's exactly the *last* thing in the world I wanted."

"Yeah, it could have been a culture tray of smallpox germs," joked Beth.

Danny simply stared at the helmet in confusion. "But Jesse doesn't wear a helmet," he announced loudly as the process of opening presents resumed full force.

"I'll bet he does now," remarked Kristen smugly.

"Will you, Jesse?" asked Danny. "Will you wear it when you play the Hawks next week?"

"Why don't you watch and see," Jesse countered.

"Aw, Jesse, you know I can't watch the game around here."

"That's true, Dan. So why don't you do me a favor and open up that flat package there, the one that's about the size of a ticket to a hockey game."

Danny fumbled for the package Jesse indicated, his eyes bright and wide. "Is it, Jesse, is it really a ticket. . .it is!"

"It sure is, buddy. I guess that means you'll just have to come and stay at my place and watch that game in person."

Danny was thrilled. Kali was enchanted. . .and in love. She knew it now as certainly as she had ever known anything in her whole life. Which was fortunate, because all of a sudden it was the one and only thing she knew for certain. Where, she wondered, did she go from here?

For the rest of the day, whenever she looked up she found Jesse watching her in a bemused, speculative way. Oh, he chatted with the assorted relatives who filtered in and out through the afternoon, and he found time to help Danny incorporate the new additions to his train set, and he dismissed the women from the kitchen after dinner with a gallant air, declaring that he certainly could be trusted alone with the good china. But still if felt as if that green-and-hot-silver gaze was always with her.

When he filled a thermos with peach brandy and asked if she'd like to see more of the thirty-odd acres of orchards and meadows the family called home, Kali didn't point out that it was too dark out to tell an oak tree from a fence post and probably very cold. She hustled upstairs to change into jeans, pulling them on over the thermal underwear Beth offered.

Jesse put his arm around her as they walked, guiding her direction with the pressure of his body. In some ways he felt closer to her than he ever had to anyone before, but there were still things he hadn't said that he wanted

to...and things he wanted to hear her say, and he knew the
still, cold night wouldn't permit them to linger long
enough to get it all in. Especially if he wanted some time
left over to hold her against his aching body the way he'd
been longing to ever since this morning when he'd rolled
from her bed. *His* bed. The thought brought a rush of fresh
oxygen to the flame he'd been fighting to control.

The only sound breaking the night's dazzling silence was
the snow crunching beneath their boots as they moved
through the backyard toward the symmetrical rows of
apple trees stretching beyond. A sliver of moonlight
worked magic on the world around them, turning the
snow to silver and the tree branches above to a sparkling
canopy of icy tendrils.

He glanced down at Kali, at the pink cheeks she was
trying to keep scrunched beneath the fleecy collar of her
jacket and at the white, misty stream of her breath rent-
ing the night air at intervals. Maybe the talking could wait
until tomorrow, he decided. He'd racked his brain all day,
trying to devise a way for them to spend some time alone
together before returning to the city and all the things that
pulled her one way and him another. Then, as he'd stood
at the kitchen sink, trying to substitute cold dishwater for
a cold shower, it had come to him in a triumphant flash—
the cabin up at Clemen's Pond where his father used to take
him ice fishing. He sure hoped Kali liked to fish.

Wordlessly he hooked his arm through hers and pulled
her more quickly through the twisting maze of trees, lifting her over a low stone wall to reach a spot he remembered from when he was a kid. It was shielded by the wall
and the natural slope of the land on one side, and on the
other by an ancient maple tree with a scarred, gnarled
lower limb that formed a perch wide enough for two.

Catching Kali about the waist, he placed her there, then swung one leg over to straddle the limb close beside her.

He pulled off his leather gloves so that he could fill the thermos cup with brandy, then flipped the thermos closed and set it in the crook of the limb behind Kali. She took the cup and sipped the same way he'd offered it, in silence.

"Thanks," she said afterward. "That helps."

"Are you too cold? Do you want to go back?" *Please let her say no*, thought Jesse.

"No. The brandy really did help."

He watched her swinging her long legs idly, and all he could think of was how those legs had felt that morning through her thin satin nightgown, and of how they'd felt even better wrapped around him when they were making love. Immediately he thrust the thought aside. If he kept this up he wouldn't get any sleep again tonight. Tomorrow and the cabin at Clemen's Pond seemed a million years away.

"Kali—"

"Jesse—" she began at the same time.

"Go ahead," he urged.

She hesitated a minute, as if stringing the words together in her head first. Then she said quietly, "I was just wondering if you really did mind about the helmet. I thought afterward that maybe I shouldn't have given it to you in front of your whole family. I mean that really put you on the spot. They all knew that you— Why are you laughing?"

He was laughing because her question led in so perfectly to what he'd been wanting to talk about all day and was having so much trouble putting into words.

"Because," he replied, "I never realized how much you use your hands to express yourself until you started to grab for the branch every few words so you won't slip off.

Here." He slid closer and put his arms around her, turning her so that her back was resting against his chest. "Is that better?"

She obeyed the persuasion of his hand moving over the curve of her hip, urging her to back in even closer. "Mmm. Much."

"Good. And I'm not upset about the helmet. In fact...I'm glad you gave it to me."

"You're glad?"

She tried to jerk around to face him, but he stilled her with a gentle hand. He liked holding her this way. And he liked the security to being able to keep his expression hidden until he knew for sure how this was going to go.

"In fact, I can't think of anything that would have pleased me more."

"But why?"

"Because it proved you care...really care. Why did you give it to me?"

She gave a small shrug. "I just wanted to. I know you said they're hot and uncomfortable, but..."

"But?" he prodded.

"But I think it's crazy for you to risk getting hurt, and..."

"And?" He wove his fingers through her hair, watching honeyed strands tumble over his skin like spun gold.

"And I don't want anything to happen to you." Her voice harbored a soft flutter.

"Because?"

He felt her lungs expand with the force of the deep breath she took.

"Because I love you."

Jesse's heart soared, and happiness began moving inside him, great lapping waves of it. Not the restless, rushing variety that usually came after winning a game. This was something very different, a feeling bordering on contentment. And he didn't have the knifing sensation in his gut, the fear that if he blinked, this would all disappear.

"Do you think it's all happened sort of...you know, fast?" she was asking. "Too fast?"

Above the clamor of his own racing senses, he heard the hesitancy in her soft voice. Belatedly, he realized that she couldn't see his stupid grin, or hear his heart hammering at the wall of his chest, and was probably waiting for him to say something.

"No, I don't think it happened very fast at all," he told her. "What I do think, though, is that your loving me is very convenient. Because..." He smiled and said the words he'd never said to any woman before. "Because I love you, too."

Kali tipped her back to look at him, and Jesse met her halfway, covering her lips that had fallen open in surprise with his own, parting them even farther in his sudden, fierce need to feel her melting beneath his touch. His fingers clenched in her hair, caging her, holding her still for a kiss that could never last long enough or go far enough to satisfy the hunger that had been building inside him. Building ever since that frozen moment in time when she'd stood by the side of the rink and, without even knowing it, challenged him with her cool, sophisticated beauty.

She wasn't cool; he knew that now. She was all velvet embers, just waiting to be brought to flame...waiting for him; as he'd been waiting for her. She wasn't even especially sophisticated. And the beauty that made the whole world stop and stare, that had caught his eye that first night and earned her the cynical edge of his tongue, was insignificant compared to all the other things she was.

Jesse swept his tongue across hers, pressing deeper. She tasted like his dreams of her, the hint of brandy on her tongue adding to the sensual flavor that was hers alone.

And she was responding exactly as she always did in his dreams...clinging, inviting, making small, yearning sounds that he wanted to turn into cries of satisfaction. He began moving his tongue into her in long, deep strokes, while his hands jerked up under her jacket to reach the softness beneath. A quiver of pleasure ran through her body when his fingers found her nipple through her sweater. It was already hard, and that made Jesse shudder in response.

For the space of several missed breaths they clung together, their bodies twisting for a closeness their awkward perch would not allow. Then Jesse forced himself to pull back. In the darkness, Kali's eyes clung to his, gleaming like black diamonds.

"I'm not backing down," he panted, his voice throbbing harshly between ragged breaths. "It's just that I'm too hungry tonight to be teased."

Her expression changed, becoming wounded, vulnerable. "I would never tease you."

Jesse cursed his insensitivity. "God, I know that, Kali. I just never should have started something I can't finish out here in the cold. But tomorrow, Kali..." The temptation of her soft mouth just inches away was too much. He touched it with his tongue once, then again, pulling away to find her smiling at his frustrated groan.

"You were saying," she prompted eagerly, "about tomorrow?"

"Right. Tomorrow..." His hands moved beneath her jacket. "How would you like to come ice-fishing with me?"

CLEMEN'S POND WAS just over the Connecticut border, a thirty-minute drive from Jesse's house. At first, when Kali had recovered from the shock of the unexpected invitation, she wondered if she should mention that she'd never been fishing before, never mind through ice, and that just the thought of sticking a hook through something alive and wriggling made her stomach flip.

Then she decided not to bother, to try looking on the excursion as a romantic adventure. After all, baiting a few hooks seemed a small price to pay to be alone with Jesse for the whole afternoon before their flight back to New York at seven-thirty that evening.

Whether she'd feel as romantic about the excursion when confronted with the hook and the squiggly victim was something she never had to find out. The first thing Jesse did when they arrived at the Spartan, one-room cabin was light a fire in the rough-stone fireplace. The second was to plop the carton she had assumed held tackle onto the counter separating the kitchen from the rest of the room. The instant he began unpacking it, Kali knew without a doubt that fishing was not what Jesse had on his mind.

"Do you always bring champagne along when you go fishing?" she inquired. Deep inside anticipation was beginning to flutter its multicolored wings.

He nodded solemnly. "Always. For the fish—the old 'dull their senses and you'll have them eating out of your hand in no time' trick."

A smile touched Kali's lips. She was falling in love all over again. The old champagne trick sounded wonderful. She wanted to ask when they could start. Instead she sat primly on the bar stool beside the counter, watching the pile beside the carton grow as he added jars of imported cheese and pâté, a smoked beef log, napkins, a radio and candles.

Her tawny brows lifted. "Candles? Will we be staying here after dark?"

"Only if you decide to forgo Saratoga Racetrack and I decided to say to hell with chasing that small black puck around an ice rink."

The trace of wistfulness in his teasing reply touched a responsive chord deep within her. "Do we have to make that decision right now?"

"No. I can think of something much more important to do now."

His smile reached out to her, familiar, reassuring, drawing from her the answering smile of a woman who knew exactly what she wanted.

Jesse leaned over the counter to bring his lips into light, delicate contact with hers. "Would you like to see what else I have in here?"

"Let me guess—a five-piece band to provide mood music? A set of black satin sheets? Various and sundry paraphernalia from the local drug store. Which isn't needed now, as you know."

His mouth crooked in a rueful smile. "Am I being that obvious?"

"Of course not—I'm just a good guesser."

"Okay, then, guess what this is." He whipped out a box about eight inches square, wrapped in gold foil and tied with a red velvet ribbon.

"A belated Christmas present," she cried. "What do I win?"

He regarded her silently, his eyes full of amused indulgence. "I'll refrain from making the obvious reply," he said finally. "Besides, I meant for you to guess what's *inside* the box."

"Then you should have given me more specific instructions."

"I'll keep that in mind as the afternoon progresses." His eyes slid over her hotly. "Now come over here and sit in my lap while you open this. Was that specific enough for you?"

"Perfect."

Besides the bar stool she was sitting on and a hassock in the far corner, the only place to sit in the entire cabin was on the brass double bed with its faded, Lone Star quilt. It had struck Kali as portentous when they'd first entered the cabin and seemed even more so now as Jesse propped his sinewy body against a pillow smack in the middle of it.

He had opened the top few buttons of his dark flannel shirt as the heat from the fire swelled to fill the small cabin. Kali's senses quickened as her eyes lingered on the triangular patch of brown flesh exposed. Just the sight of it evoked vivid memories of how it had felt to move her hands over his warm chest, brushing through the mat of soft, curling dark hairs.

"Come on, Kali," he cajoled, patting one black-denim-covered thigh invitingly. "Don't you want your present?"

Her movements were eager and sure as she crossed the few feet of worn plank flooring to stand on the braided rug near the bed. Jesse seemed to sense her mood and reached up to help her travel the final few feet, toppling her into his lap.

His breath was warm as he nuzzled her neck. "Mmm. You taste good. You always taste good," he whispered as his dark head bent, and his lips opened over hers.

She was vividly aware of the strength in the hard thighs beneath her, and of his long-boned hand coasting over her hip, causing all the muscles in her stomach to contract in a frenzy of mounting anticipation. A look that was at once lazy and enraptured warmed Jesse's green eyes as his arm curled around her, urging her closer and at the same time driving the sharp corner of the box into her ribs.

"Jesse, the box," she muttered, jerking away.

"I was getting around to that. I had no idea you were so greedy."

Kali tossed her head. "I am not greedy. I just didn't relish being impaled on my present before I even got to open it."

A slow, tantalizing smile spread across his lips, and his eyes raked her suggestively. "No, that's not quite what I had in mind, either." He offered her the box. "I guess maybe you should go ahead and open this so we can get it out of the way."

The slightly anxious catch in his voice and the intent way he watched her peel off the paper and ribbon made Kali very curious to see what sort of gift he would deem personal enough to save until they were alone to present. She parted the layers of tissue lining the box and cried out softly in delight. Inside was an elaborately detailed castle made entirely of clear, handblown glass. Only the fragile turrets, tinted the palest shade of pink, varied the dazzling crystal effect.

"An ice castle," Jesse said softly. "Every princess should have one."

Kali gazed at it, enchanted by the castle and the fact that he'd searched for something so special.

"It's wonderful, Jesse." Bright-eyed, she grinned at him. "Maybe you could bring your caveman statue over sometime, and I'll let him stand guard outside the gate."

Jesse's head shook firmly, and his fingers began stroking her throat. "No way. The caveman doesn't want to stay outside, Kali. He wants to come inside where it's warm...and soft."

Why did she have the feeling he was talking about more than a ceramic figure and a crystal castle? She was searching for the words to respond—and the breath to deliver them—when he lowered his hand to the box and lifted the castle out, holding it suspended before her so that it caught the light from the fire and sent it dancing and swirling across the dark cabin walls.

"Look inside," he said, holding her in the steady heat of his gaze.

Kali tilted her head, and for the first time noticed the gleam of something gold just inside the castle gates. With trembling fingers she pulled out a ring, the band tapered and delicate, holding a marquis-shaped diamond set at an angle and flanked by two midnight-blue sapphires.

"That," he told her softly, "is for one princess only. Mine."

Kali lifted her gaze to meet his. "Jesse...it's a diamond."

He charmed her with a playful half smile. "Please don't tell me you got a whole case of them once for doing a jewelry ad."

"No, of course not. I mean...it's a *diamond*."

"It is that." A shattered look usurped his smile. "Would you rather have something else? A pearl maybe?"

Her head shook dazedly. "Pearls bring tears."

"What?"

"Pearls bring tears," she repeated, still wearing a slightly anesthetized look. "My mother always says that."

Jesse nodded. "I see. And what do you say, Kali?"

"To what?"

"To the ring...to me."

"This always goes so much more smoothly in the movies."

"Kali, I can't understand you when you hide behind your hair and mutter. Was that a yes or a no?"

She tossed back her hair. "Neither. Before I answer I'd like to know for sure what you're asking."

His white teeth appeared in a quick grin. "I guess I did sort of overlook that one crucial detail, didn't I? Well, at least you'll know up front exactly how suave and debonair a husband you'll be getting should you decide to say yes." Setting the castle and her carefully aside, he dropped smoothly from the bed to one knee and asked in a tone that was only half teasing, "Kali, will you marry me?"

She'd had more than a hunch that the elegant ring meant exactly what she was praying it meant. Still the formally uttered question stole her breath, flooding her with excitement and serenity at once.

She answered first by slipping his ring onto the appropriate finger of her left hand and letting Jesse nudge it into place before she fell forward, her arms encircling him tightly, her lips seeking and finding the warmth of his neck, his high cheekbones, his temples...pressing an eager pattern of kisses and smiles against his skin.

"Jesse, yes, I'll marry you...I want you...oh, Jesse, Jesse."

His name fell from her lips over and over, a giddy, love-filled chant, as he tumbled her back onto the mattress and followed her down. This time there was no preliminary gentleness in his kiss, and Kali wanted none. She didn't need to be cajoled. She needed to feel their mouths fusing with fierce grinding passion as desperately as he seemed to.

"Jesse," she moaned as he broke from her with a hoarse groan. She couldn't bear to have him tease or take his time. "Jesse, please, love me—now."

His deep chuckle caressed her throat as he bent his head to focus the damp, grating attentions of his tongue and teeth on an especially sensitive spot along the side of her neck.

"That's exactly what I had planned, love."

She smiled at him, a distracted, sensual curving of her lips. "What about the fish?"

"Fish?" he echoed, his hands capturing her breasts with thrilling possessiveness.

"Mmm. You know, the ones waiting out there under the ice."

"Ah, those fish." The movements of his lower body against her grew hungry and insistent. "The fish," he pronounced, "will just have to get along without us this afternoon...."

10

"WHAT DO YOU THINK, JESSE?"

Jesse blinked and shifted his wandering attention from the kid who was winding up to throw a full-fledged tantrum in the middle of Tiffany's pricey china department. What did he think about what, he wondered.

Then, reminding himself that newly engaged men were supposed to at least feign interest in such things as whether the plate they were going to eat off for the rest of their lives had a wide silver border or a narrow gold one, he glanced at the place settings the saleslady had arranged on the counter before them.

Ordinarily he despised shopping of any kind and would have flat out refused, but it was obvious Kali wanted him to share this ritual of registering for china and crystal. For some reason, that made him more than willing to patiently endure the excursion. Patience. It was another in the string of unusual responses he was learning since falling in love with Kali.

As he continued to regard the china in confused silence, Kali fidgeted, and the elderly silver-haired saleslady finally intervened.

"Perhaps you two would like a few minutes to talk this over alone. After all, it is a big decision and—"

"No."

His slightly desperate reponse caused both women to stare at him with startled expressions. The last thing he wanted was to drag this out for the entire evening.

"I mean yes, it is a big decision," he continued fumblingly, "but no, we don't need any more time. Because it is such an important decision, I think we should stick with it until we get it settled once and for all."

He ended by pounding his hand on the counter for emphasis, then watched, cringing, as the fragile cups tottered in their saucers. The saleslady drew a deep, disapproving breath.

Jesse detected a chuckle filtering through Kali's voice, but she tried to suppress it, glancing at him warningly. "Maybe we should be looking for something more in the line of *stoneware*."

A teasing smile played around Jesse's lips as he inquired lightly, "Stone as in stone age?"

"No. Stone as in head like a," she shot back.

"As long as it's not stone as in heart like a." He skimmed the soft swell of her bottom lip with his thumb and watched her eyes turn smoky. He thoroughly enjoyed the effect his touch had on her.

"Jesse," she said softly.

"Mmm?" Jesse followed the movement of her tongue as it licked the spot he had just caressed, desire beginning to tingle through his bloodstream.

"The china," she prodded without much conviction.

"Whatever you want is fine with me," he replied in the same way. Maybe when this was over it would still be early enough to tend to what *he* wanted.

Tearing her eyes from his, she said in a voice that strained to sound normal and controlled, "I think we've narrowed it down to these two patterns."

Jesse obediently examined the pair of dinner plates and tried valiantly to form an opinion. "They're both very nice."

"But which one do you like the best?" she demanded with a trace of exasperation.

He shrugged. "I like them both."

"But what if you had to pick just one?"

"Then I'd ask you to sort of hint me in the right direction." When she didn't smile back, he let his fade and said with his finest air of decisiveness, "Let's take the gold. If we decide we don't like it in a year or two, we can always donate it all to charity and come back for the silver."

"Hockey superstars might be able to afford to toss out their china on a whim," she informed him, "but apple farmers cannot."

Jesse jerked around to face her, his eyes narrowing defensively. The dream of returning his family's acres of orchards to the glory of years past was still fragile, shared so far only with Kali.

She had been wildly enthusiastic when he had explained his plan in tentative terms that became definite as her eager approval legitimized what he'd been afraid might seem a quixotic endeavor. The once hazy dream took on color and dimension in his own mind as she interwove it with dreams of her own...dreams that seemed to mesh with his like finely tuned cogwheels.

If he'd misread her approval—or worse, if she'd been pretending—he would still love her. Nothing could ever change that. But he wanted to know upfront what kind of woman he was getting. With eyes that were intent and wary, he scoured her flawlessly beautiful face, searching for the slightest trace of derision. There was none, and ridiculous relief surged through him.

Tilting his head, he met her patient expression with a show of earnestness. "So you mean that the dishes we pick out now will be with us forever?"

Kali nodded. "For as long as we're married."

Jesse reached for her hand and enclosed it securely in his. "That's what I said...forever." He forced his gaze back to the china, mentally flipped a coin and announced, "I definitely prefer the one with the gold band. It has a more basic appeal and a certain, underlying richness."

He'd overheard and remembered more than he'd thought. The saleswoman beamed. Kali smirked, obviously not fooled in the least by his sudden display of knowledge.

"I guess that settles it," she said to the other woman. "We'll take the one with the gold rim. I gave you the list of serving pieces I'd like when I was here the other day."

As they turned to leave, Kali faced him with a challenging smile. "I had no idea you were so well informed about the subtle qualities of fine china," she drawled, "or so partial to gold, for that matter."

"The china I can definitely take or leave. But the gold..." He lifted a hand to her hair, letting it sift through his fingers like pale crystals. "Now there's a fascinating subject. Why don't we go back to your place and discuss it...intimately?"

Kali frowned in mock chagrin. "I did have a few other things on my list that we should see about."

"Did I tell you I took your advice and made a little list of my own? And at the top of it is a very crucial item— mattresses."

"We already own two."

"Exactly. Now we have to decide which one to keep." He grinned. "I think it's going to be a long process of trial and error."

"But one, no doubt, that you're feeling up to."

"I did take the liberty of devising a highly scientific way to approach the problem."

"I see." She ran her eyes over his seductively. "Do you think I might be able to give you a. . .hand with this experiment?"

Jesse released a full-tilt leer and strategically shifted the shopping bag he was carrying to the front, amazed that once again he was reacting to her like a sixteen-year-old gripped by the first, white-hot rage of desire. "I was hoping you'd offer."

The walk to the elevator seemed miles long. Issuing a silent prayer of thanks that they had it all to themselves, Jesse backed her to the wall the second the doors slid shut and spent the entire time it took to descend six floors lost in a fierce, possessive kiss.

The ride home was worse. Kali laughingly declared that he was a rotten driver even when he wasn't in heat, and that the next time he got the bright idea to conduct a scientific experiment, she was going to take a taxi and meet him back at the laboratory.

Finally he got her home, swept her off her feet as she was locking the door and headed for her bedroom. The atmosphere there was serene and softly feminine, with ruffled curtains and plump pillows covered in the same ivory satin as the coverlet draping the wide bed. Depositing her in the center of the bed, Jesse braced himself a whisper above her, feeling distinctly male and very unserene. He could almost sense waves of heat emanating from the body sprawled so temptingly beneath his, and he fought to restrain the hunger driving inside him.

It was always like this with Kali, always fevered, always urgent, whether it had been days since they'd loved each other or minutes. And always he battled his own instinctive craving for quick satisfaction and sought to pleasure her with his hands, and lips and body, bringing his love to her in gentle ways.

He was trying tonight, too, removing her clothes languorously, spending plenty of time arousing each part of her, heating her senses until they caught up with the flashfire raging through his. But tonight Kali kept getting in his way.

She interrupted his caresses to jerk his shirt off and lower his jeans. When he bent his head to kiss her breasts, she threw him off kilter with a restless twist that brought her mouth against his chest. She bit lightly, then soothed the spot with her tongue in a way that was intensely erotic. When she moved to his other side, then lower, Jesse surrendered gracefully, lost to the sensual power he had no idea she could wield so effectively.

His hips, his thighs, all of him learned the splendor of her touch, the moist, heated thrill of the kisses she bestowed with loving ferocity. The ripe resiliency of her breasts brushed against him, teasing, arousing every fiber of his being. Jesse soon felt himself losing the battle for self-control and, grasping her curled body, flipped her so she was once again lying beneath him. He knew of a way to deal with the need her sensual assault had incited...a need stronger than any he had ever known.

In a frenzy of desire, he forced her thighs apart and reached to explore the softness between, praying she was as ready as she'd made him. Instead of warm, pliant flesh, he encountered the lace barrier of the panties she was still wearing. Jesse tugged and felt the sheer material rip, a victim of his impatience. The sound made him conscious of the compulsive way he was about to make love to her, and he hesitated, torn between his will to dominate at that moment and the uncertainty that had come hand in hand with his love for her. Were you supposed to want to ravish the woman you loved?

While he wavered, Kali arched against him, bringing the dampening heat of her desire firmly against his open palm. Her expression when he worked his eyes up as far as her face was an exquisite reflection of the longing pounding inside him. Jesse smiled in the shadowy darkness. He knew then that she would welcome, not abhor, all the shades of his love—the rough along with the tender, the urgent as well as the leisurely. And he knew she wanted him right now as certainly as he knew the sun would rise tomorrow.

The knowledge thrilled him, and he was still smiling as he entered her with a hard, silken thrust and began to move in all the ways he'd learned she liked best, the ways that would quickly heat her blood and hurl them both into that velvet, blissful realm beyond satisfaction. When they reached that summit, he cried out hoarsely and covered all of her with his shuddering body, holding her tenderly as she came apart in his arms.

Reality returned to Kali first. She opened her eyes to find that the world outside her window had slid from dusk into pure, black night. She tried to orient herself in the dim light filtering in from the living room, finally deciding that the vague slipping sensation she was experiencing was definitely not a quirky aftereffect of passion.

She clutched at the wide shoulders anchoring her precariously to the edge of the bed. "Jesse, I think we're falling."

"I think I already have," he mumbled, his sweat-slick body still pressed to hers.

"You can afford to make stupid jokes—I'm the one who's going to end up on the bottom when we go."

"You liked being on the bottom...I could tell."

"Actually, I'd like to have you on the bottom—where you're completely at my mercy."

Jesse folded his arms around her and rolled so that Kali wound up straddling him provocatively. "Your wish is my command." He grinned, his teeth dazzlingly white beneath his dark mustache. "Please—be merciless."

"No," she replied after a properly contemplative pause. "You're too willing. Forewarned is forearmed and all that. I'd rather take you by surprise some night."

His grin broadened. "Anytime—I'm completely at your disposal."

"Except for the nights you have games, and the days you have practice, and all the interviews and talk shows that come between."

"You're the one who said we could work it all out," he reminded her.

"That was before I loved you, before I realized how hard it would be to get through whole days without being able to see you...touch you. And the nights are even worse." She bent to snuggle against him. "Besides, I worry about your getting hurt, Jesse."

He nuzzled his cheek against her hair. "Why? I've been wearing the helmet, haven't I?"

"Yes." The smile that formed against his hair-roughened chest faded quickly. "But now that I know how serious the problem with your knee is I worry about that." She lifted up on her hands. "Jesse, maybe that doctor is wrong about your being able to make it through the season. Maybe you should quit now and—"

"No." His tone was sharp, impatient, colder than she'd heard it since that first night in Mulligan's. Immediately he sought to gentle his expression, but the glint of implacability remained in his eyes. "Kali, love, I'll wear the helmet for you—and take all the jibes that go along with it about having a ring through my nose before I have one on my finger—and I'll trot around after you carrying shopping bags, if it makes you happy. Hell, I'd walk through fire for you, woman, but I won't quit before the season is over. I won't even discuss it."

"Whatever made me think I liked hockey?" she grumbled, collapsing on top of him once more.

His hands moved in soothing strokes along her back. "It won't be this way forever, love."

Kali's sigh ruffled the hair on his chest. "It feels like forever."

"Then let's move up the date—we can get married just as easily in January as we can in May."

"Not if we want to get married in Williston. My folks need time to plan for it, and they're definite about wanting to get to know you ahead of time, and—"

Jesse finished the thought for her in a tone of unmitigated disgust, "And the only time we can both get away to spend a few days with them is after the playoffs."

"Which brings us up to the end of March."

"Which is still a hell of a lot closer than May," he countered without missing a beat.

The dates were all familiar terrain, covered many times in the past couple of weeks, always with the same result. There was just no convenient way for them to get married before May. The head of the agency had been stunned by Kali's announcement that she planned to give up modeling and move to a small New England town no one had ever heard of—to raise apples and return to college part-time. When the woman had stopped laughing long enough to realize it wasn't a joke, she'd urged Kali to phase herself out of the business gradually, in case this "thing" with Jesse didn't work out.

Kali had agreed. Not out of any uncertainty about her love for Jesse or their future together, but because the agency had been good to her over the past five years. Anyway, she was one of their top money makers, and she owed them the professional courtesy of fulfilling the obligations they'd arranged. Getting married now wouldn't solve their problems; it would only make her a lonely, worried, married woman instead of a lonely, worried engaged one.

She explained all this to Jesse again now, patiently, for at least the tenth time, and braced herself for the explosion that miraculously didn't come. Instead, a resigned sigh rumbled deep in the broad chest she was using as a pillow.

She shot up to gape at him in feigned amazement. "What? No chest pounding? No eloquent expressions of rage at civilization in general and anything connected with glamour or fashion in particular?"

"Nope. I've thought it over, and I've decided you're right. You do have a responsibility to honor any agreements you've already made." His arms wrapped tightly around her. "But from the second you say 'I do—from this day forward,' you're mine, and your first reponsibility will be to the life we've planned together, as mine will be."

He hooked a finger under her chin and tipped it up. "I'm going to want you with me all the time," he told her with quiet certainty. "No more mints, and definitely no more posing for sports magazines."

"You don't hear me arguing. I told you, Jesse, my decision to quit modeling was made even before I met you. I just needed a good reason to go ahead with it. And you," she added in a husky drawl as her fingertips swirled across his chest with loving deliberation, "are my idea of a very good reason."

"Ah, I'm glad, because your career and my desires definitely clash." He levered up slightly, so that the tips of her breasts could continue what her fingers had begun. "I plan to be a full-time husband."

"And demanding, I hope.... "

He sank back on the bed with a teasing shrug. "I don't know about demanding. I've been doing some research, and this business of growing apples looks like hard work."

"But you and I will be working together, and if Danny accepts your job offer, we won't have to do it all alone."

"That's true." He nodded, his smile open and sincere, and a familiar sense of pride tugged at Kali's heart. The prospect of involving Danny in a business that would grow and provide security for his future was one of the aspects of Jesse's dream that pleased him most.

"And just think of all the long nights we can spend with me massaging your. . .poor. . .aching. . .muscles." She rocked on top of his hips, punctuating the softly crooned words with lavish caresses along his throat and shoulders.

"If you keep that up, my poor muscles won't be all that's aching," he growled, arching beneath her, leaving no doubt as to his meaning.

"In that case—"

The purring ring of the bedside telephone interrupted her response, but not the slow descent of her head.

"Ignore it," Jesse said.

"I don't have to—the service is on."

It rang again, just as her lips brushed his.

"Then why the hell don't they pick it up?"

"At least I thought it was on."

A third ring sent Jesse's hand up to clamp around the back of her neck. "Ignore it."

"I can't, Jess, it might be important."

"Not as important as this."

"It might be Jenny calling about Sandy—you did invite her to go riding with you again tomorrow if she could switch her doctor's appointment."

Jesse groaned and released her.

She picked up the receiver, and immediately recognized the fawning tone of Rena Maxwell, the head of the agency. At first Kali was irritated by her announcement that she had absolutely stupendous news. She could just picture Rena swiveling in her padded chair, clicking her fourteen-carat gold pen, working overtime hatching ploys to keep Kali in the stable a while longer.

But as Rena revealed her news, with an emphasis on hype and fanfare, Kali's annoyance gave way to a numbing disbelief, and finally to tingles of sheer amazement mingled with soaring excitement. She tried shrugging away from the distraction of Jesse's fingers on her breast, but he was persistent. Finally she stood and moved as far from the bed as the cord would reach, ignoring his disappointed pout.

Not so easily ignored was the fact that his pout quickly evolved into a frown; it deepened in direct proportion to her excitement. His reaction was proof positive that the silver lining Rena had just presented her with was going to float one whopper of a dark cloud over her relationship with Jesse.

But surely, she reasoned, even as she was thanking Rena profusely and saying goodbye, surely once she explained, he would understand how important this was...how it was an opportunity of a lifetime...one she couldn't pass up. She lowered the receiver to the gold filigree cradle and searched through the excited muddle of her thoughts for the best way to present the good news. Bad news to the man sprawled on her bed with silver-green fire in his eyes.

"That was Rena," she announced, absently reaching into the closet for a robe. She pulled out the red silk kimono with a vibrant yellow-and-black pattern on the sleeves and back and shrugged into it.

Jesse watched her knot the belt in silence, then lifted his dark brows a very eloquent centimeter. "Going somewhere?"

"I thought I'd make us some coffee," she replied on the spur of the moment. She could use the time alone in the kitchen to order her tumbled thoughts.

"Why? That phone call make you thirsty?"

"No." She expelled a choppy breath. "Jesse, we have to talk."

"I don't feel like talking. I feel like making love."

He stood and strode with determination around the bed. Even in the darkened room Kali could see the anger in his expression, feel it in the hands that shot out to grip her shoulders roughly.

"Jesse, don't," she said, as he bent his head.

He halted when his lips were only a fraction from hers...close enough so that she could taste his breath and feel its misty warmth. "Why, Kali?" he taunted. "Do you have a sudden headache?"

"If I do you're giving it to me," she snapped, irritation rising to mix with her anxiety.

He had no right to act so heavy-handed with her, she fumed silently. Damn, he hadn't even given her a chance to tell him about the job offer yet, much less explain it. But in her heart Kali knew she was rationalizing. Jesse obviously had garnered enough from the tone and text of her half of the lengthy phone conversation to know she and Rena hadn't been planning a church picnic.

"Jesse, listen," she began calmly. "I know you're upset..."

"Do you think I should be?" His eyes were locked on hers, charting her slightest reaction.

"I think..." She hesitated, vibrantly aware of his body pressed against hers. There was no sane reason why his standing there naked should make her feel vulnerable, but it did. "I think I was right a minute ago. I'm going to put on a pot of coffee. You might try putting on your pants."

His sardonic tone followed her out of the room. "This must be going to be one hell of a talk."

She emerged from the kitchen a few minutes later carrying mugs of coffee neither of them wanted. Jesse was standing in the windowed corner, staring out at a city that was all black velvet and glittering crystal lights. Even from the back he looked impressive—dark, hard and lean in jeans and a black cotton shirt, booted feet spread in a casual stance that belied the basic ruthlessness Kali was once again all too aware of.

He turned as soon as Kali entered the room, with an expression that told her the moments apart hadn't softened whatever mood he was in.

"Okay, Kali, let's have it." While she was still drawing a preparatory breath he continued. "I mean, how bad can it be? I could tell from your conversation with Rena that you've been offered something big. And I could tell from the look on your face as soon as you hung up and remembered I existed that I'm not going to like whatever it is at all. So shoot."

She lowered the tray to the coffeetable and rubbed her hands together, realized how jittery that made her look, so she clenched them in front of her instead. "It is big...probably the biggest and best thing that's ever happened to me—"

"Thanks."

"I meant professionally," she retorted. "Do you have to make this so difficult?"

"You're the one who's doing that."

Kali's mouth quirked ruefully. He was right. By hemming and hawing this way, she was only prolonging the agony and sending off signals that she expected him to be less than enthusiastic about the news. Maybe if she just explained the whole thing to him as if she expected him to share her excitement, he would.

Then again, maybe he would greet the whole idea with the cold disdain of which she knew he was easily capable. Hoping for the best, Kali plunged in.

"Over a month ago I was sent to do some preliminary shots for an advertising campaign that was still in the planning stages," she explained with as bright an expression as she could conjure up. "I knew it was for a new line of cosmetics, but I didn't know then who the manufacturer was or how wide a product line they were planning. Or how big the campaign itself was going to be."

The excitement she had felt while hearing the news from Rena began to stir inside her again. "The manufacturer is Colway, one of the biggest names in the cosmetic business," she explained when he still looked singularly unimpressed. "Rena said they considered hundreds of models for this job representing the new line. It will involve travelling all over the world shooting everything from magazine ads to television spots. And they picked me, Jesse," she finished in a rush of wonder. "Me—they think I personify Sizzle and Spice cosmetics."

"That pleases you?"

Kali's chin went up. "Very much. I pleases me and makes me feel very proud. I may not be as enamored of modeling as I was at first, but it is still my profession...one I've worked hard at for years. And being offered a job like this proves that I've made it to the top. It makes me even more certain that I won't ever have second thoughts about retiring. Don't you see, Jesse? After this I can leave knowing I had it all. At least I would have it all if I knew you were happy for me, too."

Sometimes during her soliloquy he'd crossed his arms in front of his chest. Now he opened them to her, and Kali nearly flew across the room to land against him with a thud.

"I am happy for you, Kali...and I'm proud as hell of you, too," he admitted, enfolding her in a rocking embrace. "And if I do say so myself, I think they made a great choice. No one, nowhere, has more sizzle and spice than my lady."

He lifted the hair from the back of her neck and gently pushed her head down to his shoulder so he could kiss the sensitive skin at the nape.

Kali giggled, feeling breathless from relief and the tantalizing movements of his lips. "I was so afraid you wouldn't understand, that we'd end up having a huge scene over this."

"Uh-uh." He lifted his head to look at her, his thumbs playing over the rapidly beating pulse in her throat. "I admit I may have reacted a little badly at first." He raised his shoulders and let them fall carelessly, smiling the slightly sheepish, slightly cocky smile she adored. "I can't help it, love. I get very upset by anything that threatens to divert your attention from me. But I'm working on it."

"Don't work too hard. I like feeling needed."

He pulled her against him. "You are needed... desperately...day and night. But if you can put up with all the separations and other inconveniences of my crazy job for another six months, I guess I can put up with yours."

The words sent a chilling unease racing through Kali, to land after a sickening wrench somewhere in the pit of her stomach.

"For twelve months," she said, purposely muffling the words in his shirt.

The tension was catching; it suddenly permeated Jesse's body, too, turning it rock hard in all the wrong places.

"What did you say?" he asked softly...too softly.

"I said for twelve months—that's how long Rena said the contract for the Sizzle and Spice campaign will run."

"Then why are we even wasting our time discussing it? It's out of the question."

With a sinking heart Kali carefully extricated herself from his hold and took a step backward. "We're discussing it because I've just been offered a very big opportunity."

Jesse snatched her hand and jerked it up so the ring he'd given her was sparkling inches from her face. "I've offered you an even bigger one...or had you forgotten?"

"Of course I haven't forgotten," she snapped, pulling her hand free. "We can still get married. In fact, this doesn't have to change our plans at all. We can still get married in May. I will get time off, you know. It'll work out perfectly."

"So we get married, and then what? What about all the traveling you said is involved in this big opportunity?"

"You'll be through with hockey by then...you could come with me."

"As what?" he demanded caustically. "Your go-for? Mr. Sizzle and Spice? No thanks, honey."

"So what do you expect me to do—just pass on this?"

"I expect you to honor the arrangements we made as scrupulously as you insist on honoring your professional obligations. I expect you to stick with our original plan to get married in May and start a new life together."

"I'm not reneging on our plans—God, Jesse don't you know how much I want that? But I want this, too, dammit. Our timetable wasn't etched in stone."

"As far as I'm concerned it was."

She tried to ignore his acerbic tone, tried to remember that this cold, hostile stranger was the man she loved more than life itself. And she did love him. She wanted to give everything to him...and she realized with startling clarity that this was the key. She wanted to *give* everything, not surrender it on demand. And she wanted him to give in return.

"Obviously we have some talking to do," she said with an ease she was far from feeling. "Why don't we sit down and try to work it out like civilized—"

"Because I'm not feeling very civilized," he interrupted roughly. "I'm feeling impatient and possessive and all those other things you find so distasteful in my character. All I want to know is whether or not you intend to take the job."

They glared at each other, standing a few inches and a million lightyears apart, waging a blistering duel with stubborn gazes. Without breaking eye contact, Kali took note of his clenched jaw, his rigid stance, and knew he would not be placated or put off. Nor would he be bartered with. He wanted no part of compromise.

He wanted unconditional surrender.

He wanted to own her.

Anger and resentment held her safely suspended above the ocean of despair that might wash over her later, giving her enough fool's courage to tell the truth regardless of the consequences. "Yes. I'm going to take the job."

For a long time Jesse looked as if someone had hit him square in the gut. Then he looked as if he might shake her into a more malleable frame of mind. When Kali felt she couldn't hold her breath a second longer, that all the nerves in her body were about to snap from being held so tensely for so long, he spoke. His voice was flat and cold, his eyes the color of the winter sea.

"Ask a foolish question..."

She watched with escalating desperation as he picked up his jacket from the sofa and headed for the door without bothering to put it on, as if he couldn't wait to get out.

"Jesse," she choked out, wanting to go to him, to touch him, but unable to move under his cold regard. "You don't have to go."

"I don't want to stay," he said simply.

Her heart stopped. She clasped her arms around her, watching her whole world collapse in slow motion. Only some shred of pride imbedded too deeply to be short-circuited by such things as emotional devastation kept her from running to him and begging him to stay.

"Fine," she said as the hand that had touched her tenderly, sensually, closed over the brass doorknob. She felt tired, colorless, cold from the inside out. "Fine. You go ahead and leave. But I hope you know that walking out just because things aren't going one hundred percent your way doesn't mean you're a man...it means you lost."

"Lost what, princess?" He whirled to face her, spitting out the name as if the feel of it on his tongue suddenly disgusted him. "A woman who'd rather be drooled over by millions than loved by one man?" His short laugh was harsh, humorless; Kali knew it would stay with her forever. "That's something I'd pay to get rid of."

KALI FULLY EXPECTED him to slam the door off its hinges as he left. He didn't. It closed slowly, with the soft brush of wood against wood...an almost silent sound, as silent as a feather drifting onto sand would be. A sound almost as final as a giant step off a rocky cliff.

He was gone.

For a long time she stood still in the shadowy silence, afraid that if she moved all the thoughts she was so carefully holding at bay would come crashing in on her. Instinctively she knew that if she allowed herself to think, she would be forced to confront the enormity of what she'd done, and that would surely snap her tenuous hold on composure.

Finally she reached to turn on the lamp beside the sofa, then all the other lamps in the room, as well as the recessed ceiling lighting in the front hall. The brightness did little to restore color to a world now cast in gray and black. But at least the activity occupied her.

After Kali returned to the living room, the first thing she saw was the tray with the untouched coffee. Two cups. Two spoons. Two carefully folded napkins. She closed her eyes, feeling a chilling wave of emptiness roll over her. She opened them again to eye the tray bleakly, not sure whether she should carry it out to the kitchen or hurl it against the wall.

It was that mood, a dark sliver that felt as if it would be embedded in her flesh forever, that trapped her somewhere between rage and loneliness. She didn't even attempt to tell herself this was simply a lovers' spat, the kind of thing all engaged couples experienced. It was much more than that. Their argument had had more than an air of finality; it had had a feeling of inevitability.

This had all happened so quickly. She'd gone from being on fire in Jesse's arms to scaling the peaks of success with Rena to watching him walk out of her life the same way he'd entered it a lifetime ago—wearing a cynical, distrustful expression. Only now that look did more than grate on her nerves—it shattered something fragile and irreplaceable deep inside her.

Crossing to stare out the night-blackened windows, she shivered from the cold that was slowly working through her from the inside out. Jesse hadn't seemed at all surprised by the job offer. Or by her desire to accept it, or by the vision of all their plans and dreams unraveling like a ball of yarn that had been too loosely wound. With an insight so sharp it sent shards of ice piercing through her, Kali realized he hadn't seemed surprised because he hadn't been. He'd been expecting this all along, and she'd been a fool not to see that.

From day one she had known he carried a chip on his shoulder about models in general and the demands of her successful career in particular. She had let herself be lulled into thinking his bias didn't really matter, deluded by the blinding force of their physical attraction and the gentler side of his personality, which he revealed in cautious bits and pieces. His attitude did matter, though it poisoned the foundation she was trying to build a future on, turning their whole relationship into a farce.

As far as Jesse was concerned, she'd started out with two strikes against her. He'd simply been waiting for the third. And it had come tonight—when she announced she was going to take the job in spite of his opposition. Torn between fury and despair, she remembered how coldly he'd rejected her plea that they talk it over. Try to find some middle ground where they could both be happy for the six or seven lousy extra months she was asking him to wait until they could begin to spin their dreams into reality. But Jesse wasn't a patient man...or a compromising one.

He was a determined man, unbending when he chose to be and ruthless when he had to be. Kali had been aware of that from the beginning, too, yet in a strange way that trait had added to his appeal. Now it frightened her, and Kali knew why. It drove home with shattering force the hopelessness of trying to salvage their love, and it erected a barrier between them that she knew she could never surmount.

As the weeks wore on her rage faded, and she was left with only the loneliness that had become as much a part of her existence as breathing...and the job she'd chosen over the man she loved. A job that now seemed more like a life sentence. Except for her Monday-night visits with Sandy, she spent her time alone, avoiding Glen's phone calls and the increasingly less tactful prying of her family, unable to summon the energy to smile or make cheerful small talk when she wasn't forced to for the camera.

Whenever she caught a glimpse of one of the Sizzle and Spice ads now appearing in dazzling variety on television and in magazines, she stared in amazement, marveling at the illusion. Anyone seeing those glossy photos of the impishly beautiful blond woman cavorting barefoot in a fountain or flirting with a host of flower-laden suitors gathered on her doorstep could easily make the mistake of thinking she was still alive.

THAT WAS EXACTLY what Jesse thought as he gazed at her, sexily smiling up at him from the pages of the magazine in his lap. He had requested the copy of *Glamour* from the flight attendant soon after they'd taken off for New York, ignoring the amusement-tainted smile she presented along with it. He sat flipping through the pages rapidly, page by page, until he found what he was looking for.

Wearing a low-cut dress that was all red satin and wide ruffles, Kali looked very much alive—the epitome of a woman in love with life, the glamorous, fast-paced life she wanted more than she wanted him. The thought never failed to bring with it a lash of pain that coiled around his chest, making it hard for him to breathe. The pain hit now as he sat there in the plane—somewhere between Kansas City and the rest of his life—and tortured himself with the slick image of what would never again be his to touch. The woman behind the image who would never again be his to love.

At first he had thought the pain would dull in time, or that he would be able to distract himself from it by summoning up the single-minded concentration on his game that had always come so easily. Yet it was as if the passing days were a whetstone, honing his misery to razor sharpness. The only thing he was distracted from was everything that wasn't Kali.

As it had once before, his preoccupation with her had interfered with his ability, during last night's game, to function. Sleepless nights and agonizingly long days had taken their toll on his reflexes, permitting a rookie from the opposing team to steal the puck right out from under his stick. Existing in a world without Kali hadn't had such a great effect on his temper, either; he'd taken off after the other player in a blind fury. The ensuing skirmish had lasted less than a minute, just long enough to get him tossed from the game for brawling. And leaving the fragile tendons in his knee completely snapped.

Jesse had hardly felt the physical pain that followed, or the emotional shock when the team physician had announced that he was through for the season, which meant he was through playing hockey forever. Thinking about it now, he realized he probably should feel crushing disappointment at seeing his shot at the Stanley Cup go up in the smoke of one stupid fight. He didn't. He felt the way he always felt these days, slightly numb, torn between a deep sense of betrayal and self-recrimination and an equally intense desire to see Kali again.

He missed her in ways he hadn't even known existed.

He missed her even before his eyes were open in the morning. He awoke, aching with the memory of the times she'd roused him from sleep with the touch of her smooth fingertips on his bare skin, or the teasing flick of her tongue across his chest.

He missed her all through the day, whenever he heard something he wanted to share with her, or saw something that would make her smile. Whenever he breathed.

Most of all he missed her at night. His bed became an instrument of torture instead of a restful haven, and he twisted on it nightly, searching for the comfortable oasis that existed only in Kali's arms.

"Pretty girl, isn't she?"

Reluctantly Jesse shifted his attention from the magazine to the woman sitting in the window seat to his right. She looked to be about seventy, petite, with carefully coiffured hair as silver as her eyes were blue. Those keen eyes were peering at him now with mingled curiosity and sympathy.

Jesse forced a polite smile. "I beg your pardon?"

"I said," the woman repeated patiently, "that she's a pretty girl." She rapped a twisted knuckle on the magazine, somewhere in the vicinity of Kali's smile.

Jesse began to flip it closed, instinctively, defensively, then realized how ridiculous that would seem and forced himself to relax.

"Yes, she is," he agreed in quiet understatement. "Very pretty."

"Well if you ask me pretty is as pretty does," countered the woman.

Jesse bit his tongue, fighting the urge to snap "Who asked you?" The time-honored cliché was one Kali had once applied to herself in the humorously self-mocking way that set her apart from all the other women he'd known.

"That's not the kind of girl a sturdy, good-looking fellow like you ought to be wasting his time mooning over," she continued.

At that moment Jesse wished fervently that he'd waited to fly back with the rest of the team in the morning. If this had been one of his teammates sitting next to him, he could at least have ordered him to shut up and mind his own business.

Instead he looked the woman square in the eye and lied. "I wasn't mooning."

"I've been watching. You were mooning." As if that settled the matter, she extended her hand and added, "I'm Lydia Sanderson."

Her frail-looking hand packed a powerful grip, and Jesse couldn't help smiling as he shook it firmly. "I'm Jesse McPherson."

"Pleased to meet you, Jesse. What happened to your leg?"

His eyebrows levered up in surprise. The flexible cast protecting his knee was well hidden beneath his gray dress slacks.

"I saw you limping as you came down the aisle," she explained, "so I know you hurt it somehow."

Jesse nodded, thinking that by the time they landed in New York, Lydia Sanderson would probably know what he'd had for breakfast, the name of his first-grade teacher and a lot of other things that were really none of her business. Somehow that didn't incur his resentment the way it ordinarily might have. Her inquisitiveness was part of a friendly, open spirit that put him at ease in spite of himself.

"I hurt it playing hockey," he said, following the brief explanation with a shrug. "Actually, I was tangling with another player."

"Tsk-tsk. Aren't you a little old for that?"

A smile spread slowly across Jesse's lips. "Yeah...yeah, I guess I am at that."

He found himself telling her all about the injury and what it meant in terms of his career and his dream of retiring as a champion. He told her about everything except how the woman in the advertisement lying beneath his hands had figured in the whole mess. His feelings about Kali were too raw to be discussed out loud...even with a woman who patted his hand as comfortingly as his own grandmother would have.

"Well, you have to look on the bright side," she advised when he finished talking.

Jesse thought instantly of Kali. "I'm not sure there is one."

"Of course there is. Those cups and trophies are all very nice, but in the end they don't add up to pile of horsefeathers. What you need," she pronounced, "is a fresh start...and a nice girl to help you make it."

Jesse nodded grimly. That sure had a tempting ring to it. Unfortunately the only girl he wanted didn't want him.

"I'm glad you agree," his new friend continued. "Because I know just the girl you need."

"You know her?"

She followed his startled gaze to the open magazine. "Not her," she said with a sneer, slapping it shut with a frown. "My granddaughter. Here—take a look."

She had the snapshot out of her purse and into his hand before he could demur. The woman in the picture was pretty, tall and slender with reddish-gold hair. She could have been a goddess—that fact wouldn't have added up to a pile of horsefeathers for Jesse. She wasn't Kali.

"Her name is Carolyn," Lydia informed him, beaming as only a grandmother can.

"She looks very...nice," he replied, returning the photo to her.

"Of course she looks nice," the woman snapped. "What's more important, she *is* nice—not all caught up with looking at herself in a mirror all the time."

"Kali's not like that."

"Who's Kali?"

He kept his eyes focused on the seat in front of him. "Just someone I used to know."

"Well, I wish you could have a chance to get to know my Carolyn. I'm sure you'd like her."

"I'm sure I would."

"She's just the kind of girl a man like you needs. She's smart...and she's a real sports fan."

Jesse nodded, an image of Kali jumping up in delight as she bested him in a sports-trivia question flitting through his mind.

"And what a sense of humor," she continued. "I swear that girl could make a stone wall smile."

Jesse's memory stirred, flashing before him scattered pictures of balloon bouquets and chocolate hockey sticks and Kali entertaining him with her version of the bump and grind...complete with knee socks and blue jeans.

"But most important, she's understanding and patient and compassionate. Those are qualities that will endure much longer than a pretty face, you know."

Jesse closed his eyes as he listened to her firm, authoritative voice, remembering the night Kali had invited Sandy along to the ballet even though she had thought he might not approve. And the day she had sat in the kitchen back home with Danny, painstakingly helping him put frosting windows on a gingerbread house.

Understanding and patience and compassion. They were important qualities, and Kali had all of them. Only he'd let the fact that she happened to be beautiful as well blind him to them. He was the one who'd been impatient and selfish and demanding.

The idea had been filtering through the fringes of his mind for weeks, but he'd refused to confront it head-on. Now it crystallized with stunning clarity. By taking this job with Colway, Kali had seized exactly the same thing he himself had wanted—a chance to go out a winner. Now, with his own hopes dashed and Kali gone from his life, he realized how little that goal had ever mattered. There was no way anyone could have convinced him of that a few months ago. Ambition could be a blinding force, and he was forced to ask himself what he would have chosen if he'd been in Kali's place...success or submission.

He closed his eyes, but doing so didn't make the answer go away. He would have chosen exactly as she had. In fact, he had refused to discuss the possibility of quitting when she'd brought up the subject of his knee. She at least had been willing to talk things over, to meet him halfway, probably even farther if he hadn't been so damn determined not to take even one step...not to bend an inch.

Unbidden and unwanted, the memory of how she'd looked and sounded that last night drifted back to him...her blue eyes glossy with hurt and disbelief and finally tears of anger, her voice trembling, begging him to talk to her, telling him how much she loved him. Like dominoes falling, his thoughts raced on...each one tripping another, more torturous memory. Kali sending him that look that could beguile and tease and arouse even across a crowded room. Kali kissing him in a way that always started out shyly and wound up setting fire to his senses. Kali responding eagerly to his caresses... shimmering out of control in his arms...staring up at him with wonder and adoration tangled in the smoky blue depths of her eyes.

God, what had ever made him think he could just walk away from her? Stupidity, he decided with a rush of self-loathing. The all-out, unwavering, pigheaded kind of stupidity he'd proved to be the master of in the past couple of months. Well, there was no reason he should change now. Going to Kali after all this time, hoping she might forgive him after the way he'd treated her, would probably turn out to be the second most stupid thing he'd ever done—but he was going to do it, anyway.

He was going to start tracking her down the second this damn plane landed and tell her that he would trade everything he owned to see her smiling at him the way she used to, and that he was willing to go anywhere and do anything as long as they were together, even if it meant traipsing around the world with her until she was old enough to model the latest in geriatric fashions.

At the flight attendant's request, he fastened his seat belt and returned his seat to an upright position—every action accomplished in the same way he nodded in response to Lydia Sanderson's continued rambling about her granddaughter...automatically. When the plane landed he carried her small tote bag as far as the terminal, then turned and handed it to her with a broad, excited grin he couldn't seem to control.

"Well, I must say, you look a lot happier now than you did when you walked onto that plane," she remarked smugly.

"I feel happier," Jesse confided, "and it's all thanks to you."

"I'm just glad I could help get two such nice young people together. I'm sure you'll like Carolyn."

Jesse was hardly listening. "I'm sure I would."

"She should be here any second now."

"That's good." Impulsively he leaned over and planted a quick kiss on her softly lined cheek. "Lydia Sanderson, thanks. I won't ever forget you."

"But my granddaughter..." she sputtered, bewildered, as he turned and started walking away. "Don't you at least want her phone number?"

Jesse barely heard. His head was full of thoughts of Kali.

"I already have it," he called back over one shoulder without breaking his oddly energetic limp.

FINDING KALI WASN'T quite the exercise in simplicity Jesse had hoped it would be. Answering-service employees, he discovered to his considerable irritation, were not susceptible to bribes, or particularly responsive to threats. He quickly pumped another coin into the pay phone and banged out the number of his friend and neighbor, Joe, hoping he might know Glen's phone number, and hoping even harder that Glen would know where Kali might be at this time on a Saturday night. He refused to consider the obvious—that she was out with another man. The thought made his heart pound dangerously close to exploding.

Joe supplied him with Glen's home phone number, then added that it probably wouldn't do Jesse much good to call him there. They had run into each other earlier, he explained, and Glen had been grumbling up a storm about having to attend some benefit tonight at the Plaza Hotel. He had mentioned something about trying to cheer up a friend and being shanghaied into making a fool out of himself in the process, Joe related with more than a hint of amusement. Joe added something about the utter humiliation of Glen's having to appear in a clown costume in public.

Jesse hung up the phone with a very triumphant grin.

FORTY-FIVE MINUTES later, Kali stepped onto the stage in the ballroom of the Plaza Hotel and began her comic routine. She had nearly forgotten about her promise to take part in this benefit for the Special Olympics. She had agreed to it months ago, before Jesse had walked away with her smile. By the time the woman in charge of entertainment had called to remind her, it was too late to back out. So she had played on Glen's concern for her, finally wheedling him into taking part in the act—a small part— so she wouldn't have to do it alone.

A few moments into the familiar routine, however, she realized her fears of falling apart had been groundless. For the first time in months she actually felt like smiling as she looked at the faces of the children in the front rows. They watched in absolute amazement as she stuck a plain white handkerchief into the pocket of her baggy-legged clown suit, only to pull out a seemingly endless rainbow of chiffon a moment later. She went quickly through the remaining stunts, chuckling at how poor Glen, disgruntled and participating unwillingly, was unknowingly aiding in the buildup to the finale, when she would chase her dour assistant from the stage brandishing a shaving-cream pie.

She had slyly refrained from mentioning that little detail to Glen during her wheedling, afraid that he wouldn't believe she intended only to toss it after him as he fled the stage, not at him. After he had seemingly botched yet another of her tricks, she shot the audience a knowing wink and extracted it from the prop box on the floor behind her. Glen took one look at the carefully mounded white foam and hightailed it off the stage even more frantically than the plan had called for.

To the roaring delight of the crowd, Kali waved a quick goodbye and took off after him, oversize shoes flapping with each step she ran, until she was off the stage and into the frantic muddle of a wild assortment of performers waiting to go on. She drew to a halt with the pie still teasingly raised, glancing left, then right for a glimpse of Glen's rented blue-and-white satin costume.

That was when she saw Jesse standing only a few feet away, one shoulder resting on the wall of the narrow backstage corridor. He was grinning at her, looking even taller and broader and more appealing than he did every night in her dreams.

Kali's senses raced. Adrenaline pumped through her bloodstream. Thought shut down, then accelerated to a dizzying speed. Slowly, free of any deliberate direction from her short-circuited nervous system, the arm holding the pie began to drop forward, propelled only by the force of gravity and fate's offbeat sense of humor.

If she'd been a few inches taller or Jesse a few inches closer, it would have landed somewhere north of his mustache-curling grin. In this case, it whitewashed the front of his leather jacket from neck to waist and a good sweep in the vicinity just below.

"I can't believe you did that," he said, slowly dropping his eyes from her face to the white globs falling from his chest like giant soggy snowflakes. "I know I deserved it, but I still can't believe you did it."

Kali couldn't believe it, either. She had fantasized a million different versions of their meeting again...she would be gracious and knock-his-eyes-out beautiful in something soft and sexy. He would be charming and contrite...and drooling. Now the big moment had arrived, and she was wearing a fright wig and a phony nose, and he was wearing a shaving-cream pie he obviously thought she'd thrown at him on purpose.

"J-Jesse," she said in a halting attempt to convince him otherwise. "I didn't—"

"You were great, honey," interrupted a tall, distinguished-looking gentleman she knew only as the balloon-animal man. He patted her on the back. "Here's a little present for you."

Kali caught the poodle made out of two intertwined pink balloons that he cheerfully tossed her way, clutching it to her chest as she turned back to Jesse. Determined to set the record straight, she took a step closer, then leaped away in shock as the poodle exploded in her too-tight embrace, sending wilted scraps of bright pink rubber wafting to the floor. The look of unholy amusement that settled over Jesse's face did nothing to soothe her nerves.

"Listen, Jesse," she began again. "I hope you don't—"

"This is all yours," announced a haughty voice as a plastic shopping bag was unceremoniously dumped at her feet.

Annoyed at the interruption, Kali glared up at a very disgruntled Glen and growled, "Not now, Glen."

"Yes, now. I want you to understand that tonight was my premiere and farewell performance as a clown—just so you won't make the mistake of ever, ever asking me to do it again." He nudged the bag closer to her with his foot. "You talked me into it, so I think it's only fair that you get to return the costume...C.O.D., of course."

"Hello, Glen," Jesse interjected, the smile he was trying to hide behind his hand evident in his deep drawl. "I loved that frantic little exit you made. Maybe someday you'll teach me how you did it."

"Sure thing, McPherson—as soon as your knee heals. I *was* sorry when I heard about it on the news last night," he added in a tone that clearly said Jessie's attitude had just changed his mind. "But at least you look as if you can still drive...which is lucky for Kali here, because she's suddenly in need of a ride home."

Kali watched him stride away in a huff, knowing he would recover before morning, then took a deep breath and faced Jesse. All thoughts of the pie and what Glen had meant about his knee fled before the rush of utter humiliation she felt at having Glen foist her off on him. She expected Jesse to be equally aghast, but he displayed a bewildering air of satisfaction. Kali parted her lips and slid a suddenly dry tongue over the parched surface.

"Don't worry," she said. "I can take a taxi home."

"I'm not worried. And you're not taking a taxi anywhere."

His voice flowed over her like warm honey, deeply masculine, achingly familiar, stirring memories she didn't want to think about while looking him in the eye.

"Really, Jesse, there's no need for you to drive me home."

He leaned closer and gently worked the red plastic nose away from her own, then peeled off her hat and hot pink curls.

"Yes, there is a need, Kali. A need deeper than any you could possibly imagine. *I* need it."

If there had been any possibility of casual conversation between them, that enigmatic remark dashed it into a million small pieces. Kali's composure was equally shattered as she grabbed her coat and walked with him to his car. She refused to let herself draw any encouragement from the way his hand lingered tentatively on the small of her back as he helped her into the low seat. She refused to believe he had come to the benefit tonight just to see her. She refused to let herself hope that after all this time Jesse had decided he wanted her.

Then what had he meant by saying he needed to drive her home? Was that the same as saying he needed her?

Kali was still wondering in silence when he parked the car in the garage and turned to her with a sheepish, one-shouldered shrug that undermined her determination not to melt at anything he said or did.

"I was hoping you'd offer me a cup of coffee."

Kali hesitated, her breath suspended as her pulse beat double-time in her throat. She would gladly offer him much more than a cup of coffee, if only she could be certain it wouldn't be tossed back in her face the next time she didn't respond to him like a puppet on a string.

"Please, Kali," he urged softly, and all her carefully constructed reasons for barring him from her life scattered like snowflakes in a brisk wind.

While Kali hung their jackets on the hall tree, Jesse stood in the center of the living room looking around with polite curiosity, as if he'd never seen the place before.

"You've made some changes," he remarked.

Kali continued to examine the dried foam streaks on his jacket. There was no way she was going to admit to him that she'd tried to sweep all traces of him from her apartment, along with the old drapes and toss pillows. Or that she'd failed.

"Nothing major. I just did a little spring cleaning."

"In February?"

She didn't even have to turn around to know that one side of his mouth had lifted in a lazy, skeptical smile. "Why not? The early bird catches the worm." She turned to him with a rueful expression. "I'm afraid your jacket is going to need an early spring cleaning, too."

"I wish you'd thought of that *before* you threw the pie at me," he said dryly.

"I didn't throw it at you."

His eyebrows darted up. "Kali, I was there—remember?"

"I know it may have looked as if I threw it, but really it just sort of"—she shrugged in embarrassment—"slipped."

He flashed her an indulgent smile. "Things slip onto the floor—not smack into the chest of someone a good head taller than you."

"But my hand was raised, and. . .oh, I don't know how it happened, but I *didn't* throw it."

"Don't worry. I already told you I deserved it. I'm just glad you have such poor aim."

Kali's flush deepened. "I didn't aim, and I didn't throw it. Jesse, I would never do something like that to you—I love you."

The words seemed to ricochet off the walls as if Kali and Jesse were standing in an echo chamber instead of her softly lit living room. Kali froze. What had she said?

"What did you say?"

Jesse's voice was raspy. Her own was suddenly nonexistent.

"I..." She shrugged, skimmed her damp palms down the front of her satin-covered legs and tried again. "I—"

"Never mind," Jesse cut in, staring at her with shock and relief and uncertainty warring in his overly bright eyes. "I like what I heard the first time."

Then he was across the room, his rough palms caging her face gently, desperately, as if she might disintegrate in his hands, like the poodle made of balloons.

"You love me." His eyes crinkled at the corners as a smile of amazement lit up his beautiful face. "You love me." His dark head bent, and his breath danced warmly across her lips. "You still love me."

"Always, Jesse," she whispered against the mouth that was only a shivering sensation away from hers. Her arms wound around his neck, urging him closer. "Always."

He kissed her as if she was a living miracle, tenderly, reverently, with a restraint Kali was too hungry to fully appreciate. Her lips parted under his, and her tongue glided over the smooth inner surface of his bottom lip in a restless invitation.

"Oh, Kali." He growled her name softly, his breath filling her open mouth in a heated rush. "I was afraid it was too late.... I was afraid you'd hate me for walking out on you the way I did."

"Never...oh, Jesse." She arched in response to the swirling caress he was lavishing along her spine.

"I was wrong, Kali, and I'm sorry." He kissed her forehead, her temples, the crest of her cheek. "I never meant to fall so hard for you, love. And it happened so quickly...filling me with feelings I didn't know what to do with." His hands roamed lower, catching her twisting hips and cementing them to his. "All I wanted to do was hold on to you as tightiy as I could. I guess deep down I was afraid of losing what I'd found with you. Instead I almost threw it all away."

Kali licked the bitter laugh from his lips. Her hands swept over his back in a wondrous touch as she relearned the pleasingly masculine terrain of hard bone and muscular swells.

"I've missed you so much, Jesse," she said, desire rippling in her husky voice. "And I love you so much."

"Oh, God, Kali, I was so scared that I'd never hear you say that again...or get a chance to say it to you. I love you, Kali."

He rested his forehead flat against hers, his eyes closed, looking years younger than he had when he'd walked in. Kali saw reflected in his face wonder and contentment that was spreading through her in hot waves, each one carrying her to a fuller awareness of how very lucky she was.

"I was scared, too, Jesse," she confessed. "But I couldn't let you make my decision for me."

A tremble passed through the strong body melded to hers. "I was a fool to walk out of here that night."

"I was a fool for signing that contract. It's ironic, but I'm already sick of the whole thing."

He lifted his head to smile reassuringly at her. "It's only for another ten months, love—not even that—and I'll be with you every single day of it. That is, if you still want to marry me."

Kali felt herself floating higher, like a kite caught in a brisk spring wind. "Of course I want to marry you— now—I mean as soon as we can. If they want to, my par-

ents can have a party to celebrate the wedding in May." A
stubborn, troubled thought pierced her euphoria. "But
you do remember that we won't be together all the time
until the hockey season is over?"

"We are going to be together every day and every
night...starting tonight." He punctuated the promise by
circling the sensitive spot just below her ear with his
tongue, releasing a gush of pleasure inside Kali that flowed
downward in a warm path.

"But what about the rest of the season? And the playoffs?" she asked lazily.

Jesse levered back, smiling the lopsided smile she
adored. "For me the season is over, Kali, as of last night.
To be more precise, hockey is over for me, period."

Kali's confused expression gave way to one of anguished concern. "Oh, no, Jesse—not because of your
knee. The morning papers all reported the injury wasn't
serious. And you're walking on it, and—"

"Shh, come here," he murmured, pulling her back close
to his chest. "It's true that it's only a mild sprain, but the
doctor said if I played on it again without having the operation, I'd risk permanent injury. Which came as no real
surprise. Hey, don't look so sad." He tipped her face up to
stare at her with loving eyes. "I'm not. Now I get to be with
you all the time."

"As Mr. Sizzle and Spice?" she asked cautiously.

He winced. "I wish you wouldn't put it quite that way."

"You can bet the gossip columns will."

"Then I'll just have to learn to live with it for a while,"
he announced with a careless shrug. "As long as you and
I know it's only for a while. And the role will have its
compensations, such as traveling with you and having
more time to sight-see than the team schedule ever
allowed."

"Are you sure that will be enough to keep you busy for the next ten months?"

"Oh, I'll have plenty to keep me busy, making plans to get the orchards back in shape." His smile gave way to a rueful expression. "I'll probably have to fly home occasionally to handle the financial arrangements for the business, but I promise I'll make the trips as brief as possible. I want to be with you always, as Mr. Sizzle and Spice, or whatever else you want me to be."

"I just want you to be you."

"Then I'm afraid you won't be getting any great prize," he said solemnly, "but at least it's something I'm good at."

"I can think of something you're even better at," she drawled, liberating the top button of his dark shirt, then all the rest.

"Oh, yeah? What's that?" His hand swept down her back to her thigh, then around and up to land, open palmed, on her belly.

Kali teased the corner of his lips with her tongue. "Not horseback riding, that's for sure—I've been getting a full report from Jenny on your progress."

"That traitor."

"Actually, she's very loyal to you. She thinks it was wonderful of you to go on taking Sandy riding even after we split up."

"It helped pass the time," Jesse admitted.

"And it helped Sandy. She's really coming along. I'm sure Jenny's told you she's started trying to ask for what she wants, and—"

"And I want to hear all about it...later," Jesse interrupted, his fingers beginning a provocative dance over her belly. "Right now I want to hear about what you think I *am* good at."

"Oh, that." With deliberate sensuality she rubbed against his pelvis, arousing herself as much as him. "Well, with your bad knee and all, I'm not sure I should even suggest something so...strenuous."

"Don't tease me, woman," he warned in a mock growl.

His hand was slipping steadily lower, sliding the satin costume against her heated flesh. Kali swayed with the force of the sensations he sent shimmering through her.

"Mmm, I love it when you call me woman," she purred, letting her head loll back, smiling up at him playfully. "Now say, 'kiss me, woman.'"

"Kiss me, woman," he repeated obediently, then jerked her to him and lowered his lips to hers in a kiss that was all the wet, wild reunion Kali had been aching for. Their tongues twisted and stroked, rediscovering in intimate detail all the pleasures of each other. When he broke away, his eyes were dark with passion, and both of them were panting for their next breath.

"How was that?" he gasped.

"Excellent...better than excellent. Now try saying, 'touch me, woman.'"

"Touch me, woman," he said in a dark, soft voice that sent pleasure rippling through her even before his hands closed over her breasts.

Excitement was shafting back and forth between them in steadily building jolts. Kali loved feeling it mount slowly, knowing it would soon lead to a dizzying surge for both of them.

"Mmm, you're a very.fast learner," she marveled as his fingers found their way beneath the wide ruffled collar and began to lower the front zipper of her costume. "Now try—"

"Kali," he whispered, the raspy edge of passion crowding the amusement from his voice. "I think I can manage to muddle through on my own from here."

"Well, if you're sure..."

"I'm sure."

The warmth of his husky words laced over her skin as he lowered the zipper completely and followed it with a moist, slow-moving tongue. When the costume had billowed to her ankles, Kali kicked it aside, smiling in anticipation as Jesse sent the wisps of her bra and panties sailing after it.

For a moment he stepped back and just looked at her with eyes that worshiped and adored and made her tremble with urgency. He reached for her, lifting her in his arms with a hoarse, impatient groan—that sharpened quickly to a pained grunt.

Wincing, he lowered her back to the floor. "You've heard that expression about the spirit being willing, but the flesh weak?" he asked, disgust in his tone. "Well, I'm afraid I'm going to have to postpone sweeping you off your feet until my knee is better."

Her eyes sparkled. "That's okay—because I fully intend to sweep you off yours tonight...and tomorrow and..."

Kali let the promise trail off as she reached for Jesse's hand. Then they were moving down the hall together, toward her bedroom, toward forever.

This month's irresistible novels from

Temptation

THE RIGHT DIRECTION by Candace Schuler

The final part of this blockbusting **Hollywood Dynasty** trilogy.

Rumour had it that renegade film director, Rafe Santana, was melting Ice Queen, Claire Kingston's, heart. Their combustible combination promised to generate more heat and hype than the movie they were working on itself. But would their affair last beyond the final take?

THE PIRATE'S WOMAN by Madeline Harper

He was standing over her when Diana Tremont regained consciousness. But her handsome, sexy, charming date was now acting like a barbarian! Adam Hawke claimed he was _Captain_ Hawke, and she was his defenceless captive...

THE SPY WHO LOVED HER by Sheryl Danson

Tough, cynical special agent Alex Sullivan thought a little assignment rescuing blonde, blue-eyed Megan Davies from a war zone ought to have been a snap. But he hadn't anticipated Megan's stubbornness, nor her warm, enticing sexiness.

MESSAGE FOR JESSE by Patricia Coughlin

The minute Jesse McPherson came into view, Kali Spencer was hooked. But what was the secret to attracting his attention? This gorgeous, impatient, _impossible_ man was avoiding her. Kali had no choice but to woo him in the most outrageous ways imaginable...

Spoil yourself next month
with these four novels from

Temptation

BODY HEAT by Elise Title

Fire, Wind, Earth, Water—but nothing is more elemental than passion.

Movie star Rebecca Fox needed to research her new role by following a real-life arson investigator—and Zach Chapin was the best in the business. But before long they were generating far more heat than the torch they were tailing…

DEAR JOHN… by Lyn Ellis

When Jenny wrote to Captain John Braithwaite, it was as a good deed. Even when their letters grew more revealing and passionate, she never thought they'd meet. But then John came home, determined to find the woman behind the words…

THE COLONEL'S DAUGHTER by Rita Clay Estrada

Casey's father had abandoned her and her mother for the Air Force. So when Casey met Major Matt Patterson she hated him for what he represented—but at the same time the dashing, sexy major was everything she could ever want…

BETRAYAL by Janice Kaiser

Allison assumed that great soul-shattering passion had passed her by—until she met David Higson and thought she'd found happiness. But instead she found herself tangled in a net of deceit, betrayal and passion so powerful that it threatened…her very life.

MILLS & BOON

Christmas Treasures

Unwrap the romance this Christmas

Four exciting new Romances by favourite Mills & Boon
authors especially for you this Christmas.

A Christmas Wish - Betty Neels
Always Christmas - Eva Rutland
Reform Of The Rake - Catherine George
Christmas Masquerade - Debbie Macomber

Published: November 1994

Available from WH Smith, John Menzies,
Volume One, Forbuoys, Martins,
Woolworths, Tesco, Asda, Safeway and
other paperback stockists.

SPECIAL PRICE : £5.70
(4 BOOKS FOR THE PRICE OF 3)